DEAD CITY

OTHER BOOKS BY ANTHONY GIANGREGORIO

THE DEAD WATER SERIES

DEADWATER
DEADWATER: Expanded Edition
DEADRAIN
DEADCITY
DEADWAVE
DEAD HARVEST
DEAD UNION
DEAD VALLEY

ALSO BY THE AUTHOR

DEAD RECKONING: DAWNING OF THE DEAD
THE MONSTER UNDER THE BED
DEADEND: A ZOMBIE NOVEL
DEAD TALES: SHORT STORIES TO DIE FOR
DEAD MOURNING: A ZOMBIE HORROR STORY
ROAD KILL: A ZOMBIE TALE
DEADFREEZE
DEADFALL
DEADRAGE
SOUL-EATER
THE DARK
RISE OF THE DEAD
DARK PLACES

DEAD CITY

ANTHONY GIANGREGORIO

DEAD CITY

ACKNOWLEDGEMENTS

This book is dedicated to my two sons, Domenic and Joseph.
Remember boys, this book proves you can accomplish anything
if you put your mind to it. And as always, to my wife, Jody.
I never say it enough so I'm going to put it in print forever.
I love you.

AUTHOR'S NOTE

This book was self-edited, and though I tried my absolute best
to correct all grammar mistakes, there may be a few here and
there. Please accept my sincere apology for any errors you may
find.

This is the second edition of this book.

Visit my website at undeadpress.com

PROLOGUE

THE WIND BLEW the waist high grass from side to side. The reeds moving like the tides in the ocean as they danced in the breeze.

Nothing but the sounds of nature could be heard on the wide open plain. Highway I-95 split the plain in two; the two lanes empty except for an occasional abandoned car or truck.

The odds of another working vehicle driving by were slim. Since the rain had come and turned the population of the world into flesh eating zombies, the production of gasoline had stopped. While there were still signs of the technology the world depended on, without electricity, many towns across America and the world had gone back to a simpler time, before man was totally beholden to its own inventions.

Where once halogen light bulbs would have lit a street or household, now there were oil lamps or simple torches.

Gone were the petty concerns that man would deal with on a day by day basis, instead replaced by the simple need to survive.

One such man was even now running for his life. Running as fast as his legs would carry him. He seemed to almost fly across the grassy plain, his feet invisible in the tall, lush vegetation.

He had been running for what seemed like days, but was in fact only hours. His feet and leg muscles throbbed from the unfamiliar exertion now being forced upon them.

Barking and growling could be heard over his shoulder and the man reached deep within him and found the energy for another burst of speed.

He had been out foraging for food for his family on the outskirts of Boston and had found himself surrounded by a large pack of wild dogs.

Since the downfall of humanity, the animals had been breeding unchecked and were now greater in number, thanks to the amount of time dogs and cats took to reproduce, as well as breeding larger litters than a human's mere one offspring at a time.

With no more animal control, the dogs had become carnivorous packs and were even now hunting him.

For the hundredth time since he had started running, Seth cursed his luck. It was bad enough to have to look around every corner or tree for a zombie, but on top of that, he now had to worry about the damn animals.

His old hunting rifle had jammed after the first shot when he'd first seen the pack of dogs and he'd taken off with feet that had felt as light as air.

Now those same feet felt like lead weights as he used the force of his will to keep them moving. The barking grew louder and he risked a quick look over his shoulder to see how close the pack was.

It was a mistake he would not live to repeat.

A roamer was lying in the field directly in Seth's path, and while Seth looked over his shoulder at the pursuing dogs, he inadvertently stumbled over the prone ghoul.

The zombie reached up with hands that resembled claws more than anything that was once human, the flesh having rotted off in the months since it had reanimated after the man who it once was, had first turned into the walking dead.

Seth never knew what happened.

One moment he was running for his life, the next the grass was flying up to hit him in the face.

The soft grass cushioned his fall and he immediately rolled over to see what had tripped him. His breath caught in his throat when he saw the rotten, maggot infested face of the ghoul.

Kicking it in the face, he felt cartilage from the putrid nose give way under his worn mountain boots.

Seconds later, he was on his feet again and running…but it was already too late! The precious time Seth had spent on the ground was more than enough for the pack of wild dogs to catch up to the hapless man, and with teeth and jaws flashing in the morning sun, they jumped onto the lone runner and pushed him to the ground.

Seth had just enough time to pull his small hunting knife from his waistband before the first dog was on top of him. His blade slashed at the dog's exposed neck, but only bit in a little thanks to the collar the German shepherd was wearing.

The animal barely noticed the shallow wound, its hunger and bloodlust in full gear.

Seth forced his arm into the dog's mouth, keeping it from tearing out his throat, but realized he was lost when another dog darted in around the first, trying for his exposed face or throat.

He screamed as another animal bit into his thigh, the sharp teeth cutting through his pants into the soft flesh beneath. His leg immediately grew cold as his warm blood soaked through his pant leg and then turned cold from the crisp November air.

He somehow was able to switch hands, his free hand now holding the knife. When the second dog dove at his face again, he slashed at its muzzle, the point of the blade just catching the dog's left eye instead.

Fluid ran out of the sliced eyeball and the animal howled in pain and backed away from the blade, but no sooner did the wounded animal move away, then two more took its place.

With his right hand still in the German shepherd's mouth, he continued slashing at the bloodthirsty animals. His vision started to fade and he struggled to overcome the weakness that seemed to be overwhelming his body.

What Seth didn't realize is the dog that had bitten into his thigh had severed a major artery and even as he continued to fight the savage animals, his life's fluid was seeping out of him with every beat of his slowing heart.

Even if he was somehow able to stand and kill all fifteen of the wild dogs, he would still be dead in a matter of minutes due to blood loss.

Seth pushed the blade of his knife into the neck of another wild dog, the animal's shriek of pain music to his ears.

Sitting in the moist earth thanks to his own blood, Seth's arm fell to the wet sod. He tried to raise the limb, but the strength wasn't there. He saw another animal's muzzle coming at his face, the dog's head blocking out the sun, but he was helpless to stop it.

The animal's teeth sank into his neck, tearing flesh and muscle to shreds.

Seth barely felt it.

His body had grown numb and his vision was gone. He was disappointed when he didn't see his life flashing before his eyes like all the movies he'd seen when he was young. Instead, he just went to sleep, while his body was torn apart and eviscerated by the ravenous dogs.

To them, he was just another animal to be devoured for food.

Once the alpha dog was finished, the other members of the pack dove in and had their fill.

The lone zombie stood off to the side, the animals ignoring it. The smell made the zombie as appetizing as eating shit to the animals.

Once all of the pack had eaten, the animals took off at a run over the plain. Cutting across the highway, they disappeared into the woods. The man was hardly enough to feed the pack and they were already on the prowl for more prey.

Behind them, the ghoul kneeled down and attempted to gnaw some small bits of meat on what was left of the man named Seth, while the tall grass continued to blow in the breeze, dancing to the rhythm of the wind.

CHAPTER ONE

A LONE GHOUL walked down the middle on the north side of Interstate 95, the sun beating down on its disease-ridden head.

The flies hovered around it, enjoying the plentiful food source, dancing and hopping like they were in some strange ballet.

The zombie walked slowly, one leg moving in front of the other. It was hungry, but then it was always hungry. The gentle breeze caressed it, smelling faintly of fading honey blossoms, as it shambled up the highway; the bright double yellow line in the middle of the road more than enough for its feeble mind to follow. It had all the time in the world and knew sooner or later it would feed.

From behind the shambling form floated the roar of an engine. Before the zombie's dead brain had even realized what was occurring, the silver Dodge Caravan was behind it.

The front grille of the van hit the body dead center, the desiccated corpse's limbs breaking apart and flying off in all directions. The torso was knocked over and then destroyed as it rolled under the undercarriage of the van. It then continued to roll for a few more feet before coming to a stop.

The flies returned within minutes, their meal still there, although in a few more pieces than before.

The van continued down the lonely highway, the zombie already forgotten.

*   *   *

An hour later, the van pulled over to the side of the road directly in front of a green highway sign that read: Boston 10 miles.

Five people stepped out of the van and onto the collected loose dirt on the shoulder of the road, their weapons out and ready.

The first man out of the van was in his late forties, his hair graying just a little, the rest a deep brown. His blue eyes took in the landscape surrounding the vehicle instantly. Satisfied for the moment they were safe, he relaxed a little and placed his Glock back into its holster on his waist. A long knife was strapped to his right leg, the sixteen inch panga more like a short sword, than a hunting knife.

The man's arms were all muscle, the hard life he now lived more than enough to burn off any excess fat, but despite all this, the man's eyes showed a kindness in them.

The man named Henry Watson still believed in mercy, and though he'd kill a man without batting an eye, he would still make damn sure the man deserved to die before he did it.

The driver hopped out of his seat and stepped out into the morning's sun. He was a young man, no more than nineteen or twenty, although the man's face said he'd learned to grow up in a hurry when the world had fallen apart.

He had a small survival knife on his hip and a shotgun in his left hand. In the back of his pants, he had placed his .38, although he preferred the shotgun.

Jimmy Cooper smiled at Henry, his teeth flashing in the sun.

"Well, old man, that's it, we're out of gas. I guess we walk."

Henry grunted. "Wouldn't be the first time," he replied as he walked to the back of the van to retrieve their backpacks.

The left side door of the van slid open and a beautiful girl of about twenty-five hopped out, her brown hair blowing in the gentle wind.

"At least we got this far, we should be able to get to Boston by late this afternoon," Mary Roberts said as she walked to the back of the van to help Henry.

Her slim figure was clearly apparent under the jeans and t-shirt she was now wearing, a light jacket wrapped around her waist. Henry smiled when she appeared next to him. The woman had been like a daughter to him since he had first met her many months ago and he would do anything to protect her.

She placed her own .38 into her pants and accepted her backpack.

She had once used a .22, but had realized the stopping power wasn't nearly enough, so had upgraded to a higher caliber weapon. Now, with the weight of the weapon in her back, she wondered how she had ever managed without it.

From the other side of the van another woman hopped out onto the shoulder of the road. Her blonde hair was tied in a pony tail and in her slacks and sweater it was clear there was a figure under her clothes any man would want.

Cindy Jansen moved to Jimmy, and when he was close enough, she placed a big kiss on his cheek. The two of them had been an item ever since Jimmy had first met her in Virginia about a month ago. For Jimmy's part, Henry had to admit he'd been nothing but a perfect gentleman. In fact, Jimmy really seemed to care for the girl.

The last passenger stepped out onto the dirt on the side of the road. He blinked up at the sun and frowned.

Jeffrey Robbins had only been with the group for a few weeks and still didn't feel like one of them. Jeffrey never wanted to take into account that he was always complaining and was never happy.

If it hadn't been for the companions, who had rescued him from his home when he had become overrun with the undead, he wouldn't even be alive to complain.

"Shit, this sucks. My feet still hurt from before we found this van and now we have to walk again? Shit." Jeffrey mumbled to himself, although he made sure it was loud enough for the rest of the group to hear.

Henry smile at that, amused at the little man. Jeffrey's five-foot four, wiry frame and thinning hair was nothing compared to Henry's almost six feet. Henry got a kick out of the little guy. Henry knew without the companions to protect him, Jeffrey would end up dead in a matter of days, so Henry had took the man on as a pet project, although he planned on losing the complainer at the first safe town they came across.

Jimmy on the other hand, hated Jeffrey and used any excuse he could to yell at the man.

"Oh, quit your whining, Jeffrey. You can stay here if you want and become lunch for a roamer then, hell, I'll even pay you," Jimmy quipped at the little man.

Jeffrey made a face that looked like he had just sucked a lemon.

"You'd like that, wouldn't you, to see me ripped apart and killed?"

"Are you kidding, it's what puts me to sleep every night with a smile on my face," Jimmy replied while pushing by the man to help Henry.

Jeffrey was about to answer when Henry spoke up. If he didn't, then the two men would argue for hours.

"All right, that's enough. Jeffrey, get all the supplies out of the front seats so we can move on. I don't like being out in the open like this," Henry told him, looking around the vehicle.

Mary placed a hand on his arm. "Why, you hear something?" She asked.

Henry shook his head no. "No, honey, I just don't like being so exposed, that's all. The sooner we're moving the better."

As if on cue, a zombie appeared out in the thick grass. It shambled towards the companions, its arms out in front of it while its hands grasped empty air. A soft moan escaped its dry and cracked lips.

Jimmy saw it first and called to Henry.

"Hey, Henry, heads up! We got ourselves a deader coming our way," Jimmy said, pointing in the ghoul's direction with his shotgun.

Jeffrey looked as well and uttered a shriek and jumped back into the van, slamming the side doors closed behind him.

Jimmy frowned. Jeffrey reminded him of Shaggy in the Scooby Doo cartoons. Except in real life the kind of cowardice Jeffrey showed could get one of the companions killed. Still, Henry said he wanted the man with them and Jimmy always deferred to Henry. After all, there could be only one cook in the kitchen.

Henry looked to where Jimmy was pointing and frowned.

Damn, he thought. Where there was one there was probably more. All the more reasons to gather their supplies and move on.

Next to him, Mary had raised her gun and was sighting the shot when Henry placed his hand on her arm.

"Wait, Mary, no gunfire if we can help it. We don't want to call any attention to ourselves out here. I'll take care of it, after all, there's only one."

"So far," Jimmy added.

"Okay, sure, Henry," Mary said, lowering her weapon.

"The rest of you continue unloading our stuff. When I finish with this one, I want to go," Henry said, moving into the tall grass to dispose of the zombie.

Henry had coined the nickname deader, as he was tired of saying zombie all the time. Whenever he saw a lone zombie it was a deader, while any zombie that would leave the cities and roam across the land looking for food, he had dubbed a roamer. As time went by, his fellow companions had picked up the nicknames also and now they seemed as natural as their own names.

When the ghoul was only a few feet away from Henry, he loosened the strap securing his panga to its sheath. When the zombie was no more than a foot away, he pulled the blade from its sheath, and in one fluid motion, sliced horizontally at the walking corpse.

The withered flesh parted like dried leather and the severed head rolled off into the tall grass, the body taking another step before falling to the ground, as well.

Henry took a moment to wipe his blade clean on the dirty clothes of the decapitated corpse and when he was satisfied his knife was clean, he replaced it in its sheath and started back to the others.

When he returned, he was pleased to see his pack on the ground at the front of the van and the others patiently waiting for him.

"Any problems?" Jimmy asked, his foot playing with a rock in the dirt.

"Nope, went down in one swipe. I like the older ones; they're easier to take down," he said, shrugging into his own backpack. "If we're ready, then let's go."

The five of them started down the highway, looking like a group going on a fun hike.

Jimmy and Cindy walked in front, holding hands. Next in line were Mary and a little behind her was Jeffrey and Henry.

As Mary walked, Jeffrey would stare at her ass. He had already made it clear to her that he liked her, but Mary wasn't interested. She had decided more than a week ago to just ignore the little man.

Henry took up the rear, constantly checking over his shoulder to make sure their back trail was clear. On top of his Glock, he had a shotgun of his own strapped to his backpack. At the moment he was out of ammunition for it and so kept it strapped to his pack. Even Jimmy only had a few more rounds left before he was empty as well. He still had a full clip for his Glock and he knew Jimmy and Mary both had full clips and at least another spare mag for their .38s.

When they had left Virginia a month ago, they had been loaded down with ammo, but it had been a hard road that had took them to where they were now. Hopefully, at the next town they found secure from the undead threat, they could barter or work for some more ammunition. If not, then they would have nothing but their hands and blades for weapons.

Not a comforting thought.

As Henry plodded onward, he could hear Jimmy yelling at Jeffrey to quit staring at his girlfriend's ass, while Jeffrey would answer something wise back.

With the bickering men in front of him, Henry kept his other ear peeled for sounds of danger, while the miles rolled by beneath his feet.

CHAPTER TWO

HENRY CALLED A halt at the junction to Route 95 and Route 93. They had already walked at least six miles and everyone was glad for the chance to rest.

There was a rusting Oldsmobile sitting in the middle of the road, just one of many other vehicles that had been abandoned at some time in the past. The closer they came to the city, the more choked with vehicles the highway became.

Henry couldn't help but wonder where all the people who had been in these cars had hoped to run to. When the contaminated rains fell, where could you hope to go except inside, where it was safe and dry? But if it was one thing he'd learned since the fall of mankind is that human beings in general would panic when faced with a threat. The public as a single entity are like lemmings running to the end of a cliff. Henry had learned early on when things had fallen apart that to remain independent was the best course of action. He also believed the only way to survive was to keep moving. The zombies were slow and as long as you continued moving, there was no way to become overwhelmed by them.

And though he enjoyed the luxury of staying in a town for some much needed rest, he and the other companions would always move on at the first chance.

His traveling companions all agreed with him… well, except for Jeffrey, and frankly, his vote didn't count.

Not long after the contaminated rains had fallen, many towns had barricaded themselves in using whatever was handy to build walls around their town. The towns became like forts where armed guards would patrol the perimeters of their borders. Sometimes they were friendly and other times they weren't.

The trick was to find a friendly one, so the companions could rest before moving on again.

Everyone sat around the Oldsmobile, while Jimmy went to the door to see if the battery was fresh or just dead like the other abandoned vehicles. Whenever the cars or trucks were abandoned, they were usually left running. They would have continued to run until the gas tank finally went dry. Then the battery would have finally drained from the ignition still being on until the vehicle became useless.

Jimmy poked around inside the car for a few minutes until he became bored. Then he went and sat down next to Cindy. The moment he was next to her, she placed her head on his shoulder. He reciprocated by wrapping his arm around her.

"What do you think we'll find in Boston?" Mary asked from the rear of the car. She had hopped up and sat on the trunk, her sneakers holding her up as they pushed on the rear bumper. She was slowly drinking from a water bottle they had refilled countless times.

Henry shrugged. "Probably the same as the other cities. The trick will be to get through the city without stirring up every deader in the place. Once we're through and on the other side, we should be fine."

"What do you mean; same as the other cities?" Jeffrey asked as he slurped down a bottle of water. Henry was about to tell the man to conserve it, but decided against it. He'd already told the man countless times and if he was too stupid to listen, then so be it.

Henry sighed and started to talk to Jeffrey like he was a small child.

"When the contaminated rains first fell the cities were hit the worst. The infected were everywhere and soon most cities became nothing more than deadlands. If you wanted to die, then going into a city was the quickest way to do it. Usually if you're quiet and stick to the main highway through the city, you can make it through without stirring up trouble."

"What happens if they hear you?" Jeffrey asked, for once listening to someone else.

Henry frowned. "If they hear you then you'll wind up having hundreds, if not thousands of those dead bastards biting at your ass."

"Did that ever happen?" Cindy asked, sitting a little closer to Jimmy.

Henry shook his head no. "No, not to us personally, but we were at a town in West Virginia and heard a few stories. Remember that, Mary?" Henry asked her.

She nodded briskly. "Oh, yeah sure, the fat man with the little woman for a wife. Yeah, they said they'd been cutting through Washington and had stirred up what to them was almost half the city. The only reason they escaped alive was because they had opened a bridge that overlooked a small river. The bridge could be opened when boats with tall masts needed to get through. They were just lucky the bridge had a backup diesel generator or they never would have made it," Mary said.

"Hell, with a wife that looked like her, he almost would have been better off," Jimmy said and received an elbow in his ribs for his trouble.

"Oww, I was only kidding," he muttered, rubbing his side with his hand and making a face at Cindy.

"You better be," Cindy said. "Even at the end of the world, we women still have to meet men's standards of what beauty should be; and that ain't right. Right, Mary?"

Mary nodded. "Hell, yeah, before you go criticizing you should take a whiff of yourself, Jimmy. You don't smell like such a great catch yourself, you know."

Henry watched the bickering; amused, until he heard a sound floating on the wind. He immediately put his hand up to signal the others to be quiet.

"What, what's the matter? You hear somethin'," Jimmy asked, studying Henry's face.

Henry walked to the rear of the car. "Get ready to move, just in case," he said, straining to hear whatever it was he'd heard repeat itself.

Then he heard it again, barking; a lot of it. That many animals didn't bode well, no matter what it meant.

"All right people, I don't know what's behind us and I don't want to find out, so let's move. Double time it, our lead is the only thing we've got goin' for us," Henry said while shrugging into the straps of his backpack.

Thirty seconds later the Oldsmobile was in their back trail, the companions moving briskly down the deserted highway.

"My feet are killing me, can't we slow down?" Jeffrey asked, askance of Henry.

"If you want to stop, then stop, Jeffrey. I'm sure whatever's behind us will appreciate it," Henry snapped at the little man. "At least you'll buy us some time while you're being ripped to shreds 'cause that many animals can't be good."

From a little in front of him, Mary looked over her shoulder. "You don't think it's what I think it is, do you?" She asked, her backpack bouncing up and down on her back.

Henry just nodded, saving his breath for jogging. "If it's dogs, then yeah, we've got problems. We need to find a place to hold up and fast."

Jimmy cursed from the front of the group. "Shit, those fuckers are fast. How many do you think there are?"

"At least ten or more," he spit back, not wanting to waste any more breath then necessary.

The miles rolled by under their shoes while the sounds of pursuit continued to grow. The pack was getting closer. The sun was high in the sky when Henry spotted what he hoped would be their salvation…if only temporarily.

About two miles outside of Boston sat a field of giant oil tanks. Full or empty, it was irrelevant right now. All Henry knew was they were close, and with only the one long, winding ladder on the side of the tank, the companions would be able to defend it from the brunt of the pack.

Moving off the highway, he took the off ramp for what he hoped was the correct exit for the tanks, the others close behind. Jeffrey was lagging behind and Henry suspected if they didn't reach cover soon, the little man would be done for.

Moving down the ramp, Henry had his Glock in his hand, the others doing the same.

"Stay sharp, people, there's got to be at least a few roamers around here," he growled out of the side of his mouth.

They were entering once populated areas again. It was just a matter of time before zombies would pop up, attracted to the noise of the companions.

Henry looked up at the afternoon sky. The clouds seemed whiter since they'd made it into New England. Henry had been wondering lately if the bacteria in the clouds would ever burn off. It had been over six months since the first infected clouds had rained down on the

Earth. Logic would reason that sooner or later the clouds would rejuvenate and the rain would be safe again. He had heard rumors that places like Antarctica and Alaska, places where it was cold, the bacteria hadn't lasted very long. His hope was that with the winter coming in New England, the clouds would clear up here as well. The only other problem was mutations. What would happen if the bacteria inside the zombies mutated and became infectious from zombie to human? So far if a healthy human became bitten by a zombie, said person would be okay, as long as they received antibiotics for the wound. But rumors had been moving from town to town about mutations. About ghouls that carried an alternate bacterium, and that if they bit you, healthy humans would turn into the undead in a matter of hours.

All this went through his mind in the blink of an eye as he jogged down the off ramp. Ten minutes later, the companions made it to the gate for the tank yard. The gate was locked, a chain wrapped around the middle. Barbed wire on the top decided the next course of action.

Stepping back, Henry nodded to Jimmy.

"Go for it," he said simply.

Jimmy nodded and pumped his shotgun. The others looked away to protect their eyes as Jimmy shot the chain securing the fence. The shotgun blast was quickly followed by the tinkling of the pieces of chain as they fell to the asphalt. Jimmy kicked the gate in and the companions moved forward. Henry paused just long enough to close the gate and wrap what was left of the chain around the gate posts. It wasn't much, but maybe it would slow the pack down for the few precious moments the group sorely needed.

They made their way across the stained cement, moving in single file, and keeping their spacing from one another. Even Jeffrey knew the time for screwing around was over. Either obey or be left behind, it was as simple as that.

When the first tank was only a hundred feet away, the first ghouls began to appear. Cindy and Jeffrey moved into the center of the group, while Henry, Jimmy and Mary formed a circle around them. Cindy had a hunting rifle she had taken from Virginia when she'd left with the companions, but she was to only use it if absolutely necessary. As for Jeffrey, there was no way in Hell Henry would ever give the man a weapon.

Moving closer to the tanks, Henry could see giant paintings on their sides. Obviously someone had at least attempted to make them more appealing to the eye.

"Head for the stairs, it's our only hope!" Henry yelled while raising his Glock and shooting at one of the first ghouls. A neat black hole appeared in its forehead, the back of its head blowing wide with a spray of blood and bone.

Mary shot at another in the crowd of undead. Her bullet struck the zombie's clavicle, the bone shattering with the impact. A split second later, half of the ghoul's head disappeared when the second bullet made itself known.

Jimmy was firing from the hip, not so much trying to kill the shambling corpses, but just slow them down long enough for the companions to make it through intact. The barrage from the shotgun sent bodies flying backwards, only to have them regain their footing and attack again.

The sound of barking filled the yard and Henry spared a glance over his shoulder at their back trail. He silently cursed at what he saw.

Almost twenty dogs had cleared the opening, their sheer body weight enough to open the gate wide. The loping strides ate up the distance and Henry knew they had mere minutes to escape or risk being torn apart by the fast moving beasts.

Man's best friend was gone, and in its place was a snarling, starving mass of muscle that wanted to feed. And Henry and his friends were the main course.

The companions continued through the few zombies left, their bullets hitting different places on the walking dead. The time for careful aiming had passed, now the only thing was to make it to the ladder of the oil tank.

Jimmy was the first to make it, and as soon as Cindy was there, the two started up the long winding ladder. The tanks were over five-stories high, the ladder's thin railing all that kept any of them from falling out into open air.

The others followed with Henry bringing up the rear. The first of the pack was only a few yards away and Henry took a quick shot into the mass of fur to hopefully dissuade them from attacking. But just as he feared, they didn't slow. As he moved up the stairs, and the pack came closer, he looked down to see one black and white-furred dog lying prone on the asphalt. Evidently his bullet had found a home after all.

The first of the pack started up the stairs, but just as Henry had hoped, only one animal could move upward at a time.

Henry smiled as he leveled his Glock at the first slavering jaws. Pausing for just a moment to get the feel for the animal's movements, he sent a bullet into its head. The expended cartridge fell out of the Glock and tumbled away to the ground below, while the first animal in line stopped as if it had slammed into an invisible wall. For a brief moment, the other dogs behind it paused, but then they simply jumped over their prone comrade and continued the hunt.

Henry was ready.

Moving backward up the stairs, he sent round after round into the dirty fur of the ravenous animals, barely slowing them down. He lined up his next shot when his Glock clicked on an empty chamber.

His clip was empty!

Cursing under his breath, he reached for his panga until an arm extended over his shoulder. A second later, the .38 in the hand sent a barrage of death into the vicious animals. The side of the tank was covered in scarlet as the blood from the animals dripped from the stairs, the wind blowing it against the painted metal.

More than half the pack was dead and the others on the stairs seemed to be rethinking if this prey was really worth it.

While the animals hesitated, Mary took the time to change clips. She ejected the spent one, quickly popped in a new one, pulled back the slide, and she was ready for more. Henry watched her efficiently change clips and had to smile. There was a time when she could barely pull the trigger without flinching.

One of the animals, a Doberman from the looks of it, started forward up the stairs. Mary lined up her shot and blew the dog's head clean off. The rest of the animal fell through the railing and tumbled to the earth, where it smashed open on impact, entrails and organs steaming in the cool November afternoon.

That was enough for the rest of the pack. With more than half their numbers slaughtered, they carefully turned and moved down the winding stairs. One of the animals slipped while trying to navigate over the carcasses on the steps and tumbled over the side. The yelping lasted for only a moment, the thud of the body hitting the pavement the end of the poor animal's cries.

Henry saw Mary had tears in her eyes and understood. It was one thing to kill walking corpses, it was quite another to kill a breathing life form that just wanted to survive the same as you.

But still, the law of the jungle remained…only the strong survive.

And today that was them.

Placing a hand on her shoulder, he started up the stairs.

"Come on, it's over, good job. You did what you had to do," he whispered.

The wind blew her hair around her face and she casually wiped her nose with her sleeve. Together, the two of them walked the rest of the way up to the roof to join the others for a much needed rest.

CHAPTER THREE

BEFORE REACHING THE top of the stairs, Jeffrey's head poked over the side. The fear clearly still on his face as his eyes scanned the area below him.

"Is it safe, did you get them all?" He asked.

Henry continued to the roof and only paused once he and Mary were off the stairs.

"Yeah, it's safe, Jeffrey, relax. Half of them are dead and the rest turned tail and ran. I still want to keep a watch out just in case, though. Thanks for volunteering, by the way," Henry said as he slapped the man on the back.

Jeffrey was about to protest until he saw the hard look in Henry's eyes. Nodding silently in consent, he sat down at the stairs, his legs dangling over the side. The wind blew a little harder for a moment and he wrapped his arms around his body to stay warm.

Satisfied that Jeffrey was done complaining for the moment, Henry walked over to the others. Jimmy had set up a small camp in the middle of the open roof of the tank and the backpacks had been laid out in a small line to use as a defense in case the pack of wild dogs had made it to the roof. Luckily, that wasn't going to be a problem.

"All set?" Jimmy asked

Henry nodded. "Should be, I think we should stay long enough to catch our breath and then we should move on. A moving target and all that."

"Agreed", Jimmy stated.

Mary walked up behind him and then fell to the roof, exhausted. "My feet are killing me," she said while taking off her sneakers and rubbing the soles of her feet.

"I hear that. I haven't had to run like that since I was in high school," Cindy piped in.

"Well, hopefully that will be the end of the calisthenics for a while," Henry said, sitting down as well. His feet were hurting, too, but he didn't want to let on. A man still had to have some of his pride, being stoic and all that.

Jimmy stood up and walked to the edge of the roof, his feet clanging on the metal. From his vantage point, a large part of Boston could be seen. The highest buildings were nothing more than blackened husks thanks to the multiple conflagrations that had burned out of control and had only been snuffed out due to lack of fuel months ago.

He had visited Boston one time when he was very young. His father had brought him there on a day trip for business, but they had still had time to have some fun and sight-see. He smiled as he remembered the fun he'd had when they rode the swan boats in Boston Common and then later they had walked through Haymarket and had gotten pizza and a fruit cup from one of the vendors.

Then they had walked out into the open area in front of the hall and had watched mimes and street artists work for tips.

Thinking back, it was one of the true real memories he had shared with his dad that was just a father and son having fun together.

He let the memories float away like smoke on the wind and refocused his watch. Boston wasn't what it once was. Now it was a graveyard, a testament to man's folly.

And the companions would soon have to run the gauntlet of its fetid streets.

Setting his jaw, he paused to look over at Jeffrey. The man was miserable. He sat there grumbling to himself about how the others got to rest and he had to stand watch. For the thousandth time, Jimmy wondered why Henry let the man stay with them. If it were up to Jimmy, he would have given the man the boot a week after they'd found him.

Moving back to Cindy's side, he sat down and stretched out. Mary was inspecting her weapon and was even now oiling and checking to make sure everything was in working order. He decided his own weapons were fine as he had just cleaned them the day before.

One of the towns they had visited previously had its own armorer and the old W.W.2 veteran had given the companions gun oil and the knowledge to clean and maintain their firearms. Without a working firearm, your time left on the Earth could be counted in days, if not hours.

Finishing her inspection, Mary placed her weapon back on her lap and leaned back against a backpack. Closing her eyes against the sun, she lay there peacefully.

With eyes still closed, she called to Henry.

"So what's our next move? Where to from here?"

Henry frowned, thinking about her question.

"Once we're rested, I say we move out towards Boston," he said. "We should be able to get in and out as long as we're quiet and keep moving; it's always worked before. Once we're further north, we'll need to find a safe place to hole up for the winter. Someplace well stocked with a solid perimeter. Maybe a hotel or a supermarket. Hell, maybe we'll get lucky and they'll be a settlement that we can stay with, it's happened before."

Mary nodded and leaned back and closed her eyes. The plan sounded feasible, plus, Henry had done well by them since they'd first met.

The four companions stretched out and relaxed, taking the time to rest up for the upcoming journey, while Jeffrey continued grumbling from the stairwell.

Jimmy heard him and smiled.

It was music to his ears.

An hour later, the companions were ready to move out. Henry took the lead down the winding stairs. The walk down was treacherous with the animal carcasses and blood spread out on the stairwell. When necessary, one of the companions would kick the carcass off the stairs to fall down to the ground.

Milling about on the ground below were five ghouls. They had seen the group climb onto the tank and had patiently waited for them to return, while a few others munched on the dead dogs, their slurping sounds of feeding floating on the wind.

Pushing another bloody body off the stairwell, Henry called up to the others.

"Don't try to kill the deaders below us, just run for it. Only shoot if they get in your way. Once we're on the ground, we'll outdistance the smelly bastards in no time. That goes for you especially, Jimmy, no target practice."

Jimmy frowned when he was called out specifically. "Yes, Dad," was all he said.

Henry was the first to the ground. With his first step on the concrete, he took off at a jog, the others close behind him.

But the ghouls would not be ignored and they came at the group with hands raised to attack.

Henry made it through the gauntlet easily, but the others weren't so fortunate.

The zombies lunged at the companions and both Mary and Jimmy fired their weapons, the .38's echoing off the tank walls. The first ghoul in the attack received a bullet in the head for its troubles. As the former shell of an oil worker fell away, Jimmy pulled Cindy with him, and the two of them ran to where Henry was waiting.

Mary was next.

One of the ghouls jumped directly in her path and she fired two quick shots. The first round struck the dead man harmlessly in the throat, the bullet passing through to become lodged in the tank wall. The second bullet was slightly higher and the man's head was blown apart by the impact of the round.

With her path clear, she ran the twenty feet to join the others.

That just left Jeffrey. If he had followed Mary after she had disposed of the zombie threatening her, then he would have been fine, but unfortunately, Jeffrey severely lacked the courage to survive in the world he now found himself in. It was only by the grace of God he was still walking around alive as it was.

Frozen in fear, the remaining three ghouls surrounded him. He let out a soft squeak and closed his eyes, awaiting his fate. He covered his head with his hands as if that would stop the brown and bloody teeth from seeking into his flesh.

While he waited for the inevitable, he suddenly heard three gunshots, one after the other. A moment later, the bodies of his attackers fell to the pavement and remained still. He opened his eyes to see Henry walking back to him, Glock raised in the air. His countenance did not look happy.

"Jesus Christ, Jeffrey, what part of run for it didn't you understand? We're already low on ammo and those three bullets could have come in handy down the line. So help me, if I had the bullet to spare, I'd put one in your damn head. Now get moving and join the others before I change my mind."

Jeffrey lowered his head and mumbled a soft thanks for saving him, then the little man jogged over to the others.

Henry double checked the area to make sure it was clear and then he too walked back to the others.

Jimmy had a wide smile on his face. "Shit, Henry, I would have let the dead bastards eat him, probably would have given them diarrhea anyway," he quipped.

"Not funny, Jimmy," Henry said while he continued past the group back toward the highway.

Jimmy looked at Cindy and Mary. "I thought it was." Then, he too, headed off.

The two women shared a silent smile, then followed the two men while Jeffrey quietly followed behind them. After walking so many feet he would quickly look around to see it was safe. He didn't know what he was more worried about, the zombies or the return of the pack of wild dogs.

Deciding both would be distasteful, he moved a little faster, until he was nearly tripping over Mary.

The afternoon sun shone down on the five companions while they continued down Route 93.

Boston was waiting and so were the undead.

CHAPTER FOUR

THE FIRST MILE into the city was uneventful. Numerous abandoned cars littered the three-lane highway, but were easy to navigate through on foot. About a half mile before Boston, there was a huge pileup on the north bound side of the highway. If they had still been in the van, they would have had to either try to drive into the city from one of the many exits to the surface roads, which would have been tantamount to suicide, or they would have had to abandon the vehicle. As it was, they all hopped the cement Jersey barriers separating the north and south sides of the highway and continued onward.

Everyone was on edge. This close to a city, it was only a matter of time before they came upon some of the undead.

Moving as quietly as possible, the group moved through the abandoned cars. Less than a mile in front of them was the edge of the city and the highway would spread out heading to points north. Hopefully, once they were through, they could scavenge another vehicle and continue north in style.

Henry noticed a reflection of the sun off of one of the buildings towering over him. He watched the light flicker in the sun, and was amused to see it moving. As if someone was raising binoculars to their eyes and then lowering them again.

"We're being watched," he said quietly to the others.

"Yeah, by who?" Jimmy inquired from his side.

"Don't know, but they're in the building over us. Could be a settlement," Henry said. "They're too far in the city to matter to us, just stay sharp in case someone up there decides to take a few potshots at us."

Henry looked to the other faces and everyone nodded. In front of them was a deep, dark tunnel. Route 93 went under the city and then opened up on the other side. This was where it became tricky. One of two things would happen, either the tunnel would be empty, the dead long gone on their search for better hunting grounds, or the tunnel would be full and they would become surrounded.

Standing at the entrance to the tunnel, Henry looked at the others.

"You ready for this?" He asked Jimmy and Mary specifically.

Jimmy held up the shotgun. "Shit, Henry, I'm never ready for this, but let's get it over with." Holding his hand out to Cindy, he pulled her closer.

Henry turned to Cindy. "Listen, honey, the key is to move fast and not to stop, no matter what. Remember, they don't move that fast, and once we're through the tunnel, we can outdistance them easily. Okay?" Henry explained to Cindy.

She nodded, clearly scared.

Henry glanced to Mary, but he knew her resolve was strong, and then Henry looked to Jeffrey.

"Let me make this perfectly clear, Jeffrey. If you fall behind, I will not be rescuing you, got it?" Henry snarled at the man.

Jeffrey nodded quickly and swallowed hard. He was scared out of his wits.

"All right then, let's go," Henry told them. "Remember, we don't need to kill them, hell, don't shoot unless absolutely necessary. One shot and the whole damn city will be on our ass." He looked at the faces surrounding him, satisfied they were as prepared as they could be.

"Fine, let's move out and stay sharp." For emphasis, Henry pulled his panga from its leather sheath. The long blade should serve him well for any stealth killing that might come along.

In a single skirmish line, the companions moved into the tunnel. The sounds of water dripping could be heard coming from off to the side. After the first fifty feet the tunnel grew dim, the light from outside only going so far to illuminate the man-made cavern. The tunnel itself smelled like a charnel-house. The end could be seen after the first thirty feet inside the gaping opening and it felt to Henry like they were walking into the maw of a giant beast.

Their footsteps echoed silently off the walls and for the moment they seemed to be the only things moving.

A rat scurried by Cindy's feet and she muffled a scream, startled by the furry rodent. Henry smiled, that was a good sign. If there were rats, then the tunnel should probably be relatively empty.

Ghouls would try to eat anything that moved.

The group walked by a few abandoned vehicles, their doors hanging open. One or two were at odd angles. The metal dented from accidents before they became abandoned.

When Jeffrey had made it past a panel truck and had continued up the tunnel, a rotten hand appeared from the rear of the truck. The rotting corpse had heard the companions and was even now slowly moving closer to the last man in line, namely Jeffrey.

As for Jeffrey, he continued onward, following Mary's back and praying to God he'd make it to the other side.

Henry detected the ghouls long before he actually saw them.

The sickly-sweet smell of rotting meat floated to his nose and made him breathe through his mouth. He looked at Jimmy and the younger man just nodded.

He'd detected them, too.

Henry turned to look at the others and used his hands to signal them they had ghouls in their midst. Through the gloom of the tunnel, he saw Mary and Cindy nod, and Jeffrey just stood there, his eyes reflecting what light was available.

Moving forward, Henry strained to hear the first signs of where the corpses could be. A hubcap or something metal was kicked across the tunnel floor as shambling feet made their way towards the companions. Henry paused, waiting to hear the sound again, but it didn't return.

With panga raised high, he moved through the maze of cars. Despite his hyper awareness, he was still taken by surprise when a dead woman jumped out at him from between a van and a truck. With a silent curse, he jumped away from her claw-like hands and swung the panga as hard as he could. The sharpened steel sliced through the neck like cardboard. The head flew off and rolled under another car and the body slumped to the ground, dead before it was fully still.

With a silent sigh of relief, he looked back to check on the others.

Jimmy smiled and gave him the thumbs up, but the others were more morose, the tension still high.

Waving the group onward, Henry started forward, hoping his was prepared if another attack came. The next attack however came from the rear as the ghoul trailing them lunged for Jeffrey's back. The man let out a piercing scream that would put any Hollywood starlet to shame. Henry and the others turned as one to see Jeffrey fighting off the zombie. The dead man was missing one arm from the elbow down, the other hand feebly trying to grab Jeffrey's body.

Before Henry could help the man, more sounds of shuffling and debris being kicked around filtered through the tunnel. Jeffrey's scream had alerted every walking corpse around the companions that they had company and that dinner was served.

Cursing his luck, Henry pulled his Glock and called out to Jimmy.

"The jig is up, his scream woke up whatever's in here with us, its time to cut and run. Stealth is no longer an option."

Jimmy nodded and grabbed Cindy's hand. Henry walked back to Jeffrey and raised the Glock. With the dead man's head in his sights, he sent a round through the top of the head, the echo of the shot bouncing off the tunnel walls and sounding like a cannon had just gone off.

Before the body had fallen half-way to the tunnel floor, Henry was already moving forward, the moans of the undead following his footsteps.

"Let's go, people, speed is our only chance!" Henry yelled.

They ran for their lives as the undead rose from under vehicles and inside trucks.

Weaving in and out of the maze of cars, Henry would push or kick any ghoul that got in his way, and Jimmy would follow that with a kick to the head. By the time the zombies regained their feet, the companions were already far away.

They moved through the deserted vehicles, relieved when the sun shone into the exit of the tunnel, but they weren't home free just yet. At least twenty-five desiccated bodies were stumbling in from the nearby exit, and if the companions wanted freedom, they had to go straight through the middle of the army of the dead.

Mary, Jimmy and Henry pulled up short and stood side by side. Then Cindy pushed in next to Jimmy and the four of them readied themselves for the slaughter to come. Jeffrey stood behind them almost completely frozen in fear.

With the sound of weapons being cocked and ammo being double checked, they began walking up the tunnel. They had been through this before. Henry stood in the middle and would take out as many in front of him as he could, while Mary and Jimmy on his left and right, would take their perspective sides as well. With luck, they would have enough firepower to break the undead line and make it through alive.

Sounds from behind them caused them to check their back trail to see more than thirty corpses walking through the lines of cars. If they didn't break through quickly, then they would be caught in between a parade of death.

As one trained unit, the four continued forward, with Jeffrey slinking at their backs.

When they were no more than eight feet from the undead horde in front of them, they began firing. Smoke filled the tunnel as the shotgun blasts and the rounds from the handguns filled the tunnel with bright flashes of light. The windshields of old cars reflected the gun fire, the flaring of light seeming like an electrical storm had gone off inside the tunnel.

Body after body fell under the barrage of bullets and the riddled corpses dropped to the ground to then become trampled by their brethren. In the space of a few heartbeats, more than half the zombies were down. Henry saw the opening and ran for it, the others on his heels. The backpack on his back bounced with the rhythm of his running as he cleared the corpses and ran out into the light. More zombies followed him and with a quick tally, he counted almost fifty before realizing it didn't really matter. Forty, fifty, either way it was too damn many to stop.

Looking to his front, the highway was clear, all the undead filing out of the tunnel.

That figured too well. When there was no food present, the walking dead usually sought out someplace dark, away from the sun.

The companions made it out into the light, and despite the horde behind them, breathed a small sigh of relief. If they were going to die, then at least it would be in the sun, not in some dark, dank tunnel.

Henry watched the undead horde moving closer and decided if he didn't stop them now, they would probably follow the companions out of Boston and beyond. So, walking over to a nearby car, he bent down and kneeled in on the asphalt.

Using his panga, he jabbed the gas tank of the car and was rewarded with a small trickle of gas. Looking up at Jimmy, he pointed to the other cars around them and Jimmy nodded, running off to do the same.

Less than a minute later, the faint smell of gas was noticeable over the bodies of the rotting ghouls.

Henry waited for the crowd to get as close as he dared, and then after he moved his friends further out of the tunnel, he lit a stray newspaper retrieved from a nearby car. Before he wrapped the paper into a tight cone, he idly noticed the headline on the front. THE DEAD WALK, CITIES DEVASTATED, more on page 1, the tagline read. Old news for an old world, he thought as he lit the tip of the newspaper. The torch lit with fervor that only dry newspaper can produce, and with a glance over his shoulder to make sure his friends were clear, he tossed the torch into the nearest, growing pool of gas.

The flames leapt up, the redolence of smoke and fumes filling the tunnel. Numerous corpses, standing directly in the pools of gas, erupted like funeral pyres. They stumbled around for a few moments and then fell to the street to be lost behind the rising flames.

The barrier was sufficient to keep the rest at bay, and with a quick glance over his shoulder to make sure the flames had done their job, Henry walked out of the tunnel and joined his friends.

Jimmy stood there, his shotgun leaning casually on his shoulder. "Shit, if only I'd brought some marshmallows, we could have had a sing-a-long."

Henry slapped him on the shoulder playfully, and with aching muscles that made him feel like he was seventy, he headed off down the road, the others walking with him. They still had a good half mile before leaving the actual city behind.

They were still a long way from home free.

CHAPTER FIVE

THE TUNNEL WAS falling away behind them as the highway rolled up and down with the terrain. Looking over his shoulder, Henry thought the tunnel looked like a fireplace, the flames crackling in the mouth, the smoke rising into the air where it was spread across the city by the gentle wind currents.

Looking forward was more promising.

The highway had been empty of ghouls. Evidently, over the past few months, they had all ended up in the tunnel and were now trapped by the roaring flames.

The sun was high in the sky and would soon start its downward progress as night set in, but until then, they had at least three more hours of light.

He could only hope they found shelter before that. Though the deadlands weren't very friendly in the daylight, the night was even less appealing.

Reaching the end of the city limits, the companions saw they now had a choice. They could continue on Route 93 or they could follow a split in the highway that would take them over the Tobin Bridge to the suburbs.

The five of them gathered in the middle of the highway and decided their fate.

"You know, I can't really say what would be a better way. If we stay on the highway, we'll be away from populated areas, but then we'll have a harder time finding food and water," Henry suggested.

Mary nodded, agreeing with him. "Yes, that's true, but if we go into the suburbs we can find an abandoned house and hole up for the night. Either that or we'll find someplace with people in it."

"Yeah, but that doesn't mean they'll welcome us, Mary. They could just as easily shoot first and ask questions later," Jimmy suggested.

Jimmy looked at Cindy and she just shrugged. "Don't look at me," she said. "I'll defer to you guys. You've been doing this stuff longer than me."

"If I could give my opinion?" Jeffrey spoke up.

"I don't want to hear anything out of you," Henry snapped at the little man. "After the stunt you just pulled I'm ready to listen to Jimmy and leave your butt here alone."

"Yeah, no shit. If you hadn't screamed like a little girl we wouldn't have had to set the damn tunnel on fire. You never block your retreat, never," Jimmy snapped.

Cindy placed her hand on his arm and Jimmy backed down a little.

A little less aggravated, he turned to Henry. "Look, old man, whatever you want to do, its fine with me." Then he and Cindy walked a few feet away and started talking softly. The words dipshit and jackass and heated glances at Jeffrey floated back. But otherwise, Jimmy seemed to be calming down.

Henry looked to Mary for some help deciding. She placed her hand on his shoulder and smiled up at his face.

"Look, Henry, whatever you decide, I'm sure it'll be fine. And if its not, then we'll deal with it, just like we always do."

He relaxed a little, the faith of his friends making him feel better.

"Okay then, I say we head over the bridge. If it doesn't work out we can always back track and head up 93."

With their destination settled, he started off down the divide. His back was killing him and the sooner they found a place to spend the night, the better.

With Henry in the lead, they set out again and just as Henry moved past a slanted eighteen wheeler with ten flat tires, a monstrosity that had once been human lunged out from the open driver's door, falling onto Henry's shoulders.

The ghoul was missing its lower half, its spinal cord swinging back and forth like a puppy dog's tail. The face was a rictus of a smile, with lips pulled back, blackened gums showing through. A gold tooth flashed in the sunlight, twinkling like a diamond in the rough, and the bifurcated corpse's white hair seemed to almost flow around its head like a halo.

Before Henry realized what was happening, the ghoul wrapped its arms around him and tried to sink its blackened teeth into his neck.

Henry spun around in a circle, taken off guard as the ghoul rode his back like a toddler at the circus. From the angle the zombie was at, he couldn't get a good grip on the squirming limbs. Teeth clacked on empty air as he tried to dodge away from snapping teeth and the overwhelming aroma of death penetrated his sinuses.

Spinning around in a circle, he realized he wouldn't be able to tear the body off him in time before fetid teeth found his flesh.

"Shoot it, for Christ's sakes, Jimmy, shoot it!" Henry yelled as he bent forward, trying to shake the ghoul off him. But the corpse was on tight and refused to let go. Henry grabbed a few fingers on the right hand and he bent them back, snapping three off like dried twigs. But the zombie felt no pain and continued to try and bite him, head snapping forward like a cobra's.

"Hold still, then, I can't get a shot without hitting you!" Jimmy screamed, fearing for his friend's life.

But Henry wasn't listening. Cold, dry breath blew in his ear and it sent a dry chill down his back. Teeth came an inch from his left ear lobe and he shook like he had ants in his pants, desperately trying to release the ghoul's death grip.

Then a shot rang out and the ghoul's head snapped forward. The left side of its skull flew off to ride the wind, then skittered across the pavement. The mottled brown and grey brain of the ghoul was exposed to the air, but it was still moving.

Cindy lowered her rifle, not wanting to risk another shot. Her shot had been excellent, but it still hadn't been enough.

Then Henry had an idea and he jumped into the air, becoming horizontal as he fell back to the hard asphalt of the highway. He was flat out, his back striking the road first and the ghoul under him was flattened, dried bones and desiccated organs flattening like an aged pancake. Limbs released his neck and he rolled to the side, coming to his feet in an instant. Before any of the companions could do anything, Henry crossed the four feet back to the supine ghoul, brought up his left size ten and a half work boot, and slammed it down on the ghoul's skull. Like a rotten pumpkin after Halloween, the head collapsed in on itself, brain matter and goo squirting out like a stepped-on ketchup packet.

But Henry wasn't finished. Pushing down on his heel, he ground the brains until they were pulp, the slimy gobbets of brain and cranium fluid coating a two foot area of the highway.

Breathing heavily, he looked up at the faces of his friends, all staring at the carnage he had wrought.

"What? The damn thing tried to eat me," he said almost apologetically.

No one answered and suddenly all four of them found something else to look at.

Scraping the sole of his boot on the rig's bumper, he turned and began moving towards the bridge, casting one quick glance over his shoulder to the others.

"You guys coming or what?" He asked almost casually, as if his life hadn't been a heartbeat away from being taken from him.

With a few furtive glances at one another, they all followed Henry, giving the brain matter a wide birth, not wanting to get any on their footwear.

With the five companions moving on, a nest of flies had already appeared, now feasting on the cooling brains glistening in the sunlight.

*　　*　　*

The walk across the bridge was uneventful, and by the time they reached the end of the long bridge, the sun was just starting to set. With dusk falling they all agreed it was time to seek shelter.

Route 1 was a three lane highway with a tall chain link fence in the middle to separate the north and south sides. Like every highway in America, the road was littered with abandoned vehicles in various states of decay. Every now and then a body could be seen inside the vehicle, the skin long dried and the bodies resembling mummies more than what they once were; living, breathing people with hopes and dreams for themselves and their loved ones.

A few shambling ghouls were seen, but they were down in the side-roads, off the highway, too far away to pose any real danger, but always watched, their position always known.

After walking past most of Chelsea, the single family homes became more plentiful. There was no more than half an hour's worth of light left, so Henry decided on a small home just off the highway. The home was surrounded by numerous other buildings, with the exception that the one he picked was directly next to the highway.

The companions climbed the six foot fence easily, only Jeffrey struggling like an aged monkey, and once they were all standing in the backyard of the house, they moved over to the back door.

Henry knocked on the back door, feeling silly, but if the home was occupied, better to find out now than when you were sneaking through the darkened house and found yourself staring down the barrel of a gun.

As for the undead, if they heard any noise, they would immediately come to the door and could be dispatched easily. If there were too many of them, they could just leave and seek out another home with hopefully less occupants.

Henry knocked again, but nothing happened. Looking to the other companions in case they had an opinion, he decided to move to the next step.

With the butt of his Glock, he broke the back door window, and after waiting another second for movement in the house, he reached in and opened the door.

Reaching into his pocket, he pulled a pen light out and clicked it on. The room was bathed in the soft glow of the tiny light and he swept it over the kitchen.

The kitchen table still had plates on it, as if the family had just left and would return in a minute, but on closer inspection it was clear the plates of food were months old.

With his Glock in his right hand and the light in his left, he moved further into the kitchen, Jimmy just behind him. Mary knew to wait outside until the all clear was given. If trouble went down, you didn't want so many people in the room you risked shooting a friend as well as an enemy.

Henry moved through the rest of the house and was pleased to find it empty.

A quick peek outside showed a few deaders wandering around, but for the moment they were harmless, unaware of the companion's closeness to them.

Henry looked at Jimmy and smiled.

"Looks like a free lunch. Why don't you go get the others and bring them in, but tell them there's a few deaders out front, so stay quiet."

Jimmy nodded and then disappeared, and a few seconds later Henry could hear the others whispering softly in the kitchen as they unpacked for the night.

Henry decided to check upstairs, just to make sure it was clear, although he was pretty sure it was empty. After all, at the first sounds he'd made, any zombies would have come running figuratively speaking.

With the sounds of the others floating up the stairs, he made his way to the top floor. The hallway was small. A bathroom was on the right and at the end of the hall were two doors, both closed and both probably bedrooms.

Making his way to the end of the hallway, he gently tapped the door with the barrel of his Glock. If something was inside, it would certainly make itself known at the sound.

He waited, his own heartbeat sounding like a locomotive in his ears. At the count of ten he turned the knob and pushed the door open.

Empty.

Grunting, he backed up a little and turned to the other door. After repeating the tapping and waiting with the same result, he opened the door and waited.

Outside, darkness had descended, the stars already coming out. Despite the darkness, though, the ambient light was more than enough to illuminate the room in a dull, suffuse glow.

Looking to the end of the room, he thought he saw a figure against the wall. It was about six feet high and had the width of a human body.

Considering the need for quiet, he pulled his panga and holstered the Glock. Then, with a deep breath, he entered the room prepared for combat.

Moving across the room, he swiped at the figure, satisfied when the blade made contact with something. Stepping back he waited, and when nothing happened, he reached for his pen light. Clicking it on, he saw he had killed a mannequin. The torso and head had on what looked like half a dress.

Looking around the room, he discovered a sewing machine in the corner and patterns for a dress on the bed. The owner of the house had been a seamstress.

Feeling silly, he backed out of the room and jumped when he felt a hand on his shoulder.

Whipping around, the panga in motion, he stopped when he realized it was Mary.

"Jesus Mary, you nearly gave me a heart attack," he said as he sheathed the long blade. "What's up?"

"Nothing, everything's fine. I just thought I'd see what you were up to, that's all. Also, I thought you'd want to know there's a cupboard full of canned food. There's more than enough for tonight and we can take the rest with us for trade or whatever."

He smiled. "That's great, come on, let's go downstairs. It's empty up here."

With a slight grin to her, he walked by Mary, and headed downstairs.

After Henry was gone, she poked her head into the bedroom with the mannequin. She saw the prone mannequin on the floor but gave it no notice, and then, she too, went downstairs.

It had been a hard road, but at least for now they could relax and take a break and just enjoy being alive.

* * *

Hours later, while the night caressed the land, the surviving wild dogs returned to the tank where so many of their brethren were slain. Time away from the men with guns and starvation had driven them back in their search of food, hunger a powerful force to dismiss.

Muzzles sniffed the dead carcasses looking for signs of life, but none were found.

Time went by, with the animals sniffing the ground, searching for the scent of their prey.

Soon the scent was found, and with a growl and a muffled bark, the first animal in line started off on the trail of the companions, the others close behind.

The hunt continued, until either the hunters or prey became rotted meat in the earth.

CHAPTER SIX

HENRY SAT QUIETLY in the front room of the quiet house overlooking the street.

He was feeling content for the first time in at least a month. The road they had traveled recently had been hard, but hopefully, now that they were in New England, perhaps their luck would change for the better.

For now his stomach was full and his friends were safe, and in the new state of things, that wasn't such a bad prospect to look forward to.

Jeffrey's snoring floated from the back room of the house, making him smile. True, the little man was a pain in the ass, but Henry had decided he'd help the man for as long as possible.

He knew why Jimmy didn't like the small man. Jeffrey was weak, and weakness in the world would get you killed. Henry thought back to when he'd first met Jimmy after the world began to fall apart. Back then, Jimmy was just a kid, fresh out of high school, now he was a hardened mercenary Henry would trust his life with, and had already on many an occasion.

Movement out on the street pulled him from his daydreaming. A trio of roamers shuffled down the street, going God knew where.

The middle one had something in its hand, and in the wan moonlight, he saw something moist and glistening. He looked away slightly, still not wanting to know what the object might be.

He watched them until they were at the end of the street and then put them out of his thoughts. If they were no threat to him then they would be ignored. There weren't enough bullets in all of New England to kill all the deaders that were out there wandering around America. Better to leave them alone and let them be.

He checked his watch in the gloom of the room. He had another hour before it was time to wake Jimmy. He was looking forward to sleep.

Hopefully, tonight, his sleep would be devoid of nightmares.

Sometimes he would dream of his dead wife Emily and of the last time he'd seen her. She had become infected and he'd had to kill her with a frying pan in their kitchen. He tried to remember how she looked before that fateful day, how her smile would always brighten up a room, and he defied anyone not to chuckle along side her when her sing-song laugh filled a room.

But she was dead now, like so many others.

Sometimes he wondered if maybe they were the lucky ones and he and his friends were the unfortunates.

A creaking of floorboards called his attention to the ceiling. In the rooms upstairs, Mary was in one room and Jimmy and Cindy the other. Earlier in the evening, he had heard the latter two making love, and with the exception of just a little jealousy, Henry had been happy for them. It was nice to see people finding happiness in each others arms while the world was filled with death and misery.

The creaking grew louder and he could hear someone walking down the stairs.

Despite knowing it was a friend walking down those stairs, Henry's hand still hovered over his Glock, old habits refusing to be ignored.

"Hey, Henry, it's me, Jimmy," the young man's voice floated from the shadowy figure at the bottom of the stairs.

Henry placed his hand on his lap and relaxed.

"Hey, Jimmy, what are you doing up? You've still got another half hour before it's your turn," Henry whispered in the dark.

He could imagine the smirk that was probably crossing Jimmy's face as he answered.

"Yeah, I know, but to tell you the truth, I'm pretty wired."

"Oh yeah?" Henry asked. "Wouldn't have anything to do with you and Cindy earlier, would it?"

Jimmy was only a foot in front of Henry now, and with the wan light sliding in from the window, Henry could see the embarrassment on the younger man's face.

"Oh, you heard that huh?" He asked.

"Yeah, I'm afraid so, in fact, I bet the whole city heard you two. Relax its fine. I'm glad you've found someone."

"Thanks, Henry, that means a lot," Jimmy answered.

Silence settled between the two men, until Jimmy spoke up.

"If you want, I'll take over a little early for you."

Henry's face lit up a little. "Yeah? Hey that'd be great. It's been quiet, a few roamers outside, but they kept walking."

Jimmy nodded, waiting for Henry to get up. Jeffrey's snoring bounced off the walls and Jimmy frowned.

"Great, don't tell me I've got to listen to that for the next two hours."

Henry patted Jimmy on the back. "Sorry, pal, try to ignore it. Well, good night."

"Night, Henry," Jimmy said as he peeked out the front window to survey the street.

Henry moved off to the living room. There was a medium sized couch with his name on it, and after paying a visit to the bathroom, the tub was where they had been leaving there remains as there was no running water, he did just that.

As soon as his head hit the frilly throw pillow, he was out, secure in the knowledge Jimmy had his back, while Jeffrey's snores floated through the house, threatening to wake the dead from their graves…if there were any still in them.

*   *   *

Upstairs, Mary rolled over in the bed she was presently occupying, bed springs squeaking softly in the night. She had slept a little, but the ghosts of the house continued to haunt her.

The room's walls could just barely be seen in the dull gloom, the open shade of the bedroom window more than enough to illuminate the room slightly.

On the walls were pictures of the high-school girl who had once called this room home. Pictures showed the pretty blond girl in her cheerleading uniform and there were others where she was with a boy, probably her boyfriend, Mary assumed.

On the nightstand were brochures for colleges. Mary had glanced through them earlier, imagining the hopes and dreams of the young girl, now all destroyed.

Lying back in bed with a sigh, she stared at the ceiling, taking stock of her life and where it might go; wondering where she'd be in six months or a year; or even if she'd still be alive. Life was so fragile now. All it took was another human being with a reason to kill you and you could wind up dead. No repercussions, no justice…only vengeance.

And she knew her friends would do just that for her if she died through foul play.

That made her feel a little better in an odd sort of way, knowing she had people at her back who cared about her. Henry had become like a father to her and Jimmy had become the brother she had never wanted. Hell, no sister would want a brother like Jimmy. He would drive them all crazy.

She chuckled at that, thinking of the young man. Jimmy always had something to say, usually an inappropriate remark at the worst time, but that was what made him endearing. Not that she would ever tell him that.

All the thinking was making her tired again. She had learned not to try and think to hard anymore, just to take one day at a time and see where it led.

From outside her window, a forlorn howl carried on the wind, the source of the sound still quite a distance away. Rolling over on her side, she closed her eyes and tried to think of better times when the world was full of promise, and before she realized it, she was fast asleep.

CHAPTER SEVEN

THE NEXT MORNING, the companions rose from their beds at first light. Despite the fact there were no alarm clocks anymore; the companions had learned to rise with the sun.

Mary was on watch when Henry, Jimmy and Cindy walked into the front room of the house.

"Morning, guys, how'd you sleep?" Mary asked from the window. The night had been uneventful, the street staying quiet and empty with the exception a few wandering ghouls.

Scratching his head while entering the room, Henry looked at Mary with sleep still in the corners of his eyes.

"About what you'd expect," he grunted and promptly fell into a small love seat in the corner of the room.

"Not me, man, slept like a baby," Jimmy said.

"Oh yeah? Didn't sound much like sleeping to me," Mary joked.

Jimmy turned beet red and mumbled something about using the bathroom. Cindy just smiled, not embarrassed in the least. That was fine with Mary. That was what she liked about the girl.

Jeffrey was still snoring in the back room.

Mary looked to Henry. "Want me to go wake him up?" She asked.

"Nah, let him sleep. It's not like we need him for anything," Henry said, feeling a little better as his blood started to flow. Luckily, it wasn't that cold outside and the house was comfortable, most certainly better than sleeping outside by a long shot.

"So what's the plan? What's next?" Mary asked from the window.

Henry leaned back in the love seat, his face creasing as he thought about it.

"Well, I figure we should just stay here for another day, at least until we're rested, then we'll move on. See what's down the road. There's got to be people once we get away from the city limits. And hopefully they'll be friendly."

"And if their not?" Jimmy asked, walking back into the room.

"Well, then I guess we'll just have to keep moving north."

The four of them stayed quiet, letting it all sink in, each in his or her own thoughts. With winter coming, they needed to find a place to stay, or else risk freezing to death. The home they were now in was fine for a day or two, but as a long term shelter it was hopeless. There was no way to defend it when the numbers of the dead grew around the house, and the numbers would grow just as soon as the rotting corpses discovered there was fresh meat inside.

"All right, folks, off you go. Go find something to do. We'll stay here till tomorrow morning and then we'll move out," Henry said, waving the others away.

Jimmy looked to Cindy and flashed her a lecherous grin. "I know how we can kill an hour or so," he said, his grin growing wider. Cindy smiled back and looked to Mary and Henry with a raised eyebrow, almost like she was asking permission.

Henry waved them away. "What are you looking at me for? Go do what you want."

"Okay, thanks, Henry," she said, following Jimmy.

Jimmy glanced over his shoulder at Henry as he walked up the stairs.

"Just yell if you need me, Henry," Jimmy called.

"Don't worry, I will, just keep it down, okay?" Henry asked.

Jimmy waved agreement and then disappeared up the stairs. A moment later the dull thud of a bedroom door slamming shut filtered down the front room.

The sound of the door closing woke Jeffrey up and he stumbled into the front room, his pants a little larger in front than when he had gone to bed.

"Well, well, look who decided to get up," Henry said as he raised himself to his feet.

"Looks like he's not the only one up," Mary joked as she watched Jeffrey.

Jeffrey stood there in the middle of the room, not quite awake. Then he glanced down at where Mary was looking and saw he had a serious case of morning wood. Turning away from the woman, he smiled bashfully.

"My apologies, my dear, I had no idea," he said timidly.

Mary smiled as she stood up and headed for the kitchen.

"Don't worry about it, Jeffrey, I was only joking. I've had boyfriends, you know."

"Oh, yes, of course," he said to her back as she moved away. Then he proceeded to the bathroom to take care of business.

A moment later he returned with a sour look on his face.

"What's the matter with you?" Henry asked, as he sat down in a chair in the kitchen.

"Did you see the bathroom? My God, that's disgusting," Jeffrey said, referring to the bathtub

"Oh, yeah? What would you prefer? To go outside and get your ass bit off while you're taking a dump? Get over it, once we leave this place, it'll be empty. It's not like whoever lived here is coming back," Henry said.

Jeffrey sat down at the table across from Henry and frowned. "Well, it's still gross, that's all I'm saying."

"Fine, duly noted," Henry said. "Now shut up and eat breakfast."

Breakfast consisted of bottled juice and dried cereal. The cabinets were full and it was going to break Henry's heart to have to leave some of it behind. But just as it wasn't good to have too little, if you overloaded yourself, you'd end up restricting movement and that half second might mean the difference between life and death. So, for the time being, he told everyone to eat up and enjoy the large amount of food at their disposal.

Jimmy and Cindy came down from upstairs and the five companions sat around the kitchen table talking about the future and miscellaneous things.

Jimmy had done some exploring and had found a lock box under the bed in the room he was staying in. After a few whacks from the butt of his .38, he'd managed to get the small container open. Inside, he'd found a .357 Smith and Wesson revolver with a box of .50 caliber shells. The gun smelled of oil, and when Jimmy had inspected it, he seriously wondered if the weapon had ever been fired. Now the weapon sat in the middle of the table, ignored, while the companions talked of other things.

When breakfast was over, everyone went off in different directions in the house, each doing chores to keep occupied.

Jeffrey found a deck off cards and passed the time playing solitaire, while Henry striped and cleaned his weapons again, dry clicking to make sure all the springs and pins were working efficiently.

Jimmy did the same to his armaments and Cindy helped. Then Jimmy helped Mary with her .38; striping the weapon to pieces and then reassembling it.

Later, Henry went exploring in the basement, checking to see if there was anything they could use. He found a seven inch hunting knife and decided to spend the next hour honing his skill at throwing it long distances. A few weeks ago, at one of the small settlements the companions had stayed at, he had befriended a man who had served in the Army. The man had shown Henry how to flick the knife and impale an enemy from across the room. Henry knew he needed practice, so after setting up a few cardboard boxes, he had started throwing the knife from across the cellar. He only stopped when the poor quality blade had snapped off at the tip from striking the cement cellar floor one time too many.

Mary investigated the upstairs rooms a little more, the feeling of being an intruder returning. She shrugged it away as inconsequential and continued scavenging. She found a change of clothes almost identical to her own size and changed out of her old ones. With new underwear, socks, shirt and pants, she felt like a new woman. After she finished, she found a few things for Cindy if the girl felt like changing. Looking around the room she'd slept in the night before, it didn't seem so oppressing in the light. Finishing up, she decided to go back downstairs to see what the others were doing. When she stepped into the hall, sounds of lovemaking drifted through the door of Jimmy and Cindy. Smiling bashfully, she slowly crept past the door and headed downstairs.

There was still more than half a day left of light and then the night to deal with. While it was nice to be able to relax, she'd be glad to leave this place behind her and the old ghosts that resided within it.

*   *   *

A few miles away, the pack of wild dogs, thirteen strong, wandered through the tunnel where Henry had made the firewall. The fire was long out, the flames extinguished once the gas was exhausted. A few of the vehicles still smoked; the heat hot enough to melt the glass on the windshields on some of the vehicles.

The animals struggled to find the scent of the humans who were their prey, but the smoke and fumes made it difficult.

Working their way through the charred and blackened corpses, they would sometimes have to jump aside from the flailing hands of the shattered dead who were still active, but the animals were too quick for the surviving ghouls.

Eventually, one of the dogs picked up the scent of their prey on the other side of the tunnel, the trail easier to follow now that the animal was away from the residual smoke and fumes.

Moving slowly, so as not to lose the scent, the starving animals moved down Route 1.

The pack was patient and knew soon they would find their prey. And when they did, they would feast on the fresh meat of the humans.

CHAPTER EIGHT

NIGHT WAS FALLING on the second day spent in the abandoned house. The companions had already packed their gear, the backpacks sitting on the kitchen floor. The plan was to get a good night sleep and then head out at the crack of dawn.

Checking his watch, Henry saw the time was a little past five, the street already shrouded in darkness. The days were shorter in New England, he remembered, looking out onto the dilapidated street.

Luckily, it was quiet tonight, nothing but a few cats playing tag on the sidewalk to break the solitude of the night. Watching the houses across the street, he couldn't help but wonder what skulked around in the basements and darkened hallways, just waiting to come out and feed.

Sitting back in his chair, he smiled ruefully.

Not tonight fellas, he thought. If all goes well, we'll be out of here in the morning with none of you knowing we were ever here.

Jeffrey's raised voice pulled him from his reverie. The others were playing poker in the kitchen, a small candle the only illumination.

He hadn't felt like playing and so had volunteered for the first watch. Now, hearing the fun they were having, he thought he might have made a mistake.

A shadow drifted by the dark exterior of the house, causing Henry to sit up in his chair. The shadow had been to low to the ground to be a ghoul, unless it had no legs, the rotting corpse pulling itself along by its hands only.

Besides, it had glided across the window almost gracefully, not slowly crawling like a slug or worm.

He waited for any signs the shadow would reappear, and after a full five minutes had passed uneventfully, he decided he must have imagined it.

Leaning back in the easy chair, he relaxed and listened to his friends arguing about the poker game.

*   *   *

The clock read six as Henry stood to stretch, his back muscles flexing from the exertion. The poker game had ended a few minutes ago and Jimmy and Cindy had already gone back upstairs for another bout of love making.

Ah youth, he thought.

He remembered when he could go three times a day, too. But those days were long ago. Well, maybe that long ago.

Mary and Jeffrey were still sitting at the kitchen table. They were talking softly about something Henry couldn't hear.

A soft thumping floated down from upstairs from the vicinity of Jimmy's room and so Henry didn't hear the sound of razor-sharp claws on the cement in the front and back of the house.

Without warning, the glass in the upper portion of the kitchen door shattered and shadowy forms burst into the room.

Jeffrey was so startled he fell over in his chair, his head striking the ceramic tile covering the kitchen floor. Mary had jumped to her feet, but was knocked over as a heavy figure covered in fur forced her to the floor by the sheer weight of its body.

Henry heard the sound of breaking glass from the other room, but before he could act, the front window exploded inward, shards of glass filling the room in a glistening spray of crystal splinters.

Raising his arm over his face by instinct alone, he avoided losing an eye in the onslaught of razor-like, glass daggers, a few sticking into his jacket coat and just slightly piercing the skin beneath.

Before he knew what was happening, large forms of varying colors shot through the open window to land inside the room.

The initial shock gone, Henry moved his arm from his eyes to see the front room of the house filled with a pack of wild dogs. For the moment, the animals stood still, sizing up their prey before attacking, no growls issuing from their throats. Henry had his hand hovering over his Glock, but knew with the first flinch he made, the animals would be on him.

He may get the first one that chose to attack him, but by then the others would be on top of him, and there was no way he'd be able to fend off that many claws and teeth.

Mary's screams floated through the house and he knew he had to do something before the woman was hurt.

His hand went for his Glock, while at the same exact moment the first animal in line saw his movement and lunged for Henry's throat. Henry already knew he wouldn't be fast enough to get his weapon between him and his attacker, but he'd be damned if he wouldn't go down without a fight.

What seemed like slow motion to Henry, but actually happened in a blink of an eye, was that while the animal was in flight, its fangs ready to attach themselves to his throat, and Henry was pitifully too slow on the draw to shoot the animal, the dog seemed to stop in mid-air, and was then thrown across the room to land on the couch against the wall; its innards covering the fabric in a crimson spray.

Half a heartbeat later, a shotgun blast filled the room, and Henry looked over to the stairs to see Jimmy with the barrel raised, already sighting another animal in his gun sights. Not wanting to waste the precious seconds Jimmy had given him, Henry brought up his Glock and shot the next animal in front of him.

The side of the shaggy dog's fur exploded when the round connected, the animal screeching to the world its pain. Jimmy had already fired again, catching two other dogs in the shotgun's spray. The barrage peppered the sides of their hides and the animals shrieked in pain.

This wasn't how it was supposed to happen; the dog's should have burst in and ripped the humans to bloody shreds, the animals thought to themselves, as their heads looked for a way out of the house, but it was too late. Henry moved in front of the shattered front window and raised his weapon.

There would be no escape. Either man or dog would die tonight and no mercy spared for either.

In quick succession, Henry and Jimmy slaughtered the remaining animals, ten in all, until they was nothing left but twitching, bloody forms on the floor of the house.

With the dogs down, Henry was already moving towards the kitchen, knowing Mary and Jeffrey were in there. Mary was still on the floor, her hands under the muzzle of the large German shepherd on top of her. Her hands were already sliced by the animal's teeth as it continued to try and rip her throat out. She managed to pull one hand away and she frantically searched the floor for something to use as a weapon; anything would due at this point. Then her hand brushed the polished metal of the .357 that had fallen from the table top.

The gun had toppled to the floor when the animals had attacked and Mary frantically tried to grab the handle of the weapon, her fingers just out of reach.

With one more stretch of her arm, she was able to pull the gun closer. Her hand wrapped around the grip and she pulled it up and under the dog, the nose of the weapon buried in the chest of the snarling animal.

Thanking God, Jimmy had taken the foresight to load the weapon when he'd brought it down to show everybody, she squeezed the trigger. The gun moved slightly in her hands, but the animal continued snarling over her. Panicking, she squeezed the trigger two more times, the dog's internal organs shredding apart in the path of the bullets. The third bullet continued out of the back of the animal and became lodged in the ceiling of the kitchen, pieces of plaster trickling down to fall on the shredded back of the animal

The animal shuddered as the trauma it had received finally overwhelmed its bloodlust. It collapsed on top of Mary, the other dogs in the kitchen still trying to get at her flesh, but unable due to the pile of dead meat covering her.

Jeffrey was in the corner of the kitchen. Two smaller dogs had him cornered and he was using a straw broom to keep them at bay, but the dogs were growing impatient and would soon attack in force; overwhelming the little man.

Henry and Jimmy charged into the room, weapons at the ready. After only a moment to take in the scene, they both started to systematically shoot the animals, the small room a disadvantage to the dogs. The speed the attacking pack so relied on was useless in the close quarters of the room and in a matter of seconds all the animals were down, either dead or ready to climb on the last train headed west.

Henry leaned down and pulled the carcass off Mary, his heart in his throat, imagining what he'd find under the bloody, matted hair.

Mary's blue eyes looked up at him, her breathing coming heavily, thanks to the dead weight of the animal. He helped her to her feet and hugged her.

Noticing the blood on her shirt, he was about to ask how she was when she nodded no, she was fine.

"It was the dog's blood. I think I'm fine," she said, checking herself for wounds. With the exception of a few deep scratches on her hands and arms she had made it out of the attack in one piece.

"Hey, what about me?" Jeffrey said in a high pitched voice.

Jimmy gave the man a once over and snorted. "I'll think you'll live, tough guy."

Cindy's voice floated down the steps. "Is it okay to come down now?"

Jimmy looked over his shoulder at the carcasses strewn on the front room's floor.

"Yeah, if you want to, just pay attention to the ones on the floor, I'm not sure if they're all dead."

"That's okay, I'll stay up here until you need me; just give me a call," Cindy said and then moved back up the stairs.

For the first time, Henry really looked at Jimmy's attire. The young man was wearing nothing but one sock and his boxer shorts.

Henry smiled. "Nice outfit," he smirked.

Jimmy looked down at himself and then back to Henry.

"Would you have preferred if I'd taken the time to get dressed?"

Thinking back to the close call from a moment ago, he shook his head. "Hell, no, good point."

A moan floated in through the front window and Henry looked to see what it was, although he already knew. About five of the undead were at the front window, for the moment not sure how to gain entry.

Henry looked over their shoulders into the darkened street and could see more shadowy figures moving towards the house.

"Shit, I knew this would happen. Every goddamn deader in town heard those gunshots. If we don't move quick, we'll be up to our asses in rotting corpses in no time."

Nodding, Jimmy turned to head back upstairs. "Got it, I'll get Cindy and we'll be right down." Then Jimmy took off at a run, his bare feet slapping on the tile until he was on the carpet of the stairs.

Henry turned to Mary, but she was already on top of things. The companion's packs and other gear were already on the kitchen table, ready to go.

"Great job, Mary. I want us out of here and on the road in less than five minutes."

Henry moved back to the front of the house, careful not to trip on the carcasses littering the floor. The smell of blood, feces and urine filled the room, almost enough to make him gag. But over time he had grown accustomed to the smell of death, though he hated to admit it.

A few of the ghouls had become adventurous and were trying to climb through the shattered front window. Henry raised his Glock and shot the closest ones away. The zombie's heads snapped back and the bodies fell away. Whether they were dead for good or just disabled was irrelevant for the moment.

One of the undead placed its hand on the shattered glass frame of the window. The razor shards sliced the hand in two, the loose skin causing the hand to sway back and forth as the ghoul struggled to gain entry. Henry turned away, disgusted. For the moment, they were okay, but within another fifteen minutes there would be more walking dead than they had bullets.

Jimmy and Cindy came running down the stairs. Jimmy was now dressed and so was Cindy. Each of them was wearing new coats that had been looted from a hall closet. Cindy had an extra set of clothes for Mary.

"Once we're away from here, I'll give them to her," the blonde girl said.

Henry nodded and headed for the kitchen.

"All right, people let's move. Out the back and back onto the highway. The first place we can find, we'll hold up for the night and then continue on in the morning."

As one, the companions gathered their gear, just as a crash filtered in from the front of the house. Jimmy ran and checked, returning seconds later.

"They're in," he said simply.

Henry nodded and opened the back door which led out into the backyard. The light from the stars gave everything an ominous look, shadows seeming to be everywhere. There was a crash from the side of the yard and Henry ran and poked his head around the corner of the house. The small wooden fence separating the front of the house from the back was now flat on the ground; the ghoul's crushing it under their feet as they explored the exterior of the house, looking for food.

The companions moved across the small lawn and climbed the tall fence separating the house from the highway just as the zombies charged into the backyard. They howled and moaned at the companions, mouths slavering like the wild pack of dogs had done only minutes ago.

Their meal was so close, but had escaped.

Jimmy walked up to the chain-link fence, the fingers of the ghouls pushing through the links, trying desperately to reach him. Jimmy spit into the closest one's face, the spittle following the contours of the corpse's cheek until it dripped off to fall into the grass below.

"Not this time, assholes," Jimmy said, the hate in his voice apparent. Then he turned and walked to the rest of the group waiting for him on the road, and with one last glance at the shadowy figures, started up the highway; the moans of the undead following him for longer than he would have liked.

CHAPTER NINE

FIVE PEOPLE WALKED in the middle of Route 1 as the clouds drifted by overhead; their silhouettes framed by the stars. Their packs were heavy, weighted down with the supplies taken from the house.

Henry had them walking in a loose skirmish line, so as to make a more difficult target for anyone watching in the night. He was fairly confident they were alone in this part of the city, but to become lazy could get them all killed.

The house they had abandoned was more than two miles away and Henry was already searching for a possible temporary shelter for the night. The highway was littered with abandoned cars, the doors thrown open wide to let in the elements. One car had a family of squirrels living inside, and as the companions came up to the vehicle, the small animals inside made clear their discontent.

The group backed away and moved on.

About a mile down the road, a large Greyhound bus was sitting on the debris encrusted shoulder. As Henry walked closer to large vehicle, he was able to make out that the front left tire was flat. All the windows seemed to be intact, however, and when he stopped and took a better look around their surroundings, he was pleased to see they were most definitely alone on the abandoned highway.

Jimmy saw him eyeing the large bus and walked up to stand next to him.

"What're you thinking?" Jimmy asked.

Henry frowned, although in the shadows of the highway, Jimmy wasn't able to see his face very well.

"I'm thinking that if that's empty, we can stay there for the night," Henry said, gesturing to the bus.

"And what if it's not empty?" Jeffrey asked from behind him.

Henry turned and looked at the little man, his face set in stone.

"Then we make it empty," he stated.

Henry and Jimmy moved to the door of the bus while the others stayed in the middle of the highway. If Henry's plan fell apart, then they would all need to hightail it away from the large vehicle.

Jimmy pushed the large accordion like door in with his left hand. The hinges squeaked quietly in the dark, but to the two men it sounded like a siren.

"Sorry," Jimmy whispered to Henry. Henry nodded and waved the man forward.

They had already picked who would go in first by a game of rock, paper, scissors.

Henry had won thanks to the fact that Jimmy always picked rock.

Jimmy placed his right foot on the first step, the bus creaking softly with his weight. He winced at the sound and waited a heartbeat, but when nothing happened, he continued inside.

There was the faint smell of decay inside the bus, but nothing to signal there was a presence of any of the walking dead. Slowly, Jimmy stepped up the next step until he was looking over the seats into the bus, Henry right behind him.

There were thirty-six seats, eighteen to a side. Jimmy started walking down the aisle, expecting something rotten and putrid to jump out at him and try to bite his face off. He was more than halfway down the aisle when he noticed something on one of the seats.

Henry saw him pause and called to him.

"What's wrong, what do you see?" He whispered.

Jimmy held up his hand for him to wait a second and then Jimmy leaned over and retrieved something. Henry walked down the aisle to investigate when Jimmy turned to him and smiled in the gloom of the bus.

"Thought you might need an extra hand," he quipped, holding a severed hand in front of him by the few stray threads of blue cloth still clinging to the wrist.

Henry stepped back for a second and his face grew hard.

"Cut it out, Jimmy, let's make sure this place is secure before you start screwing around."

Chastised, Jimmy apologized, then cracked open a window on the shoulder side of the bus, and dropped the hand outside to land in the dirt.

Checking the rest of the bus went more quickly after that, Henry helping with the search. The last place to check was the bathroom in the back of the bus, so Henry stood in front of the small door and tapped on it with his knuckles. If there had been something inside, it would have immediately tried to get out and attack the two men, so Henry was fairly certain the bathroom was empty.

He was wrong.

With his Glock in his hand, he opened the door to discover the desiccated corpse of the bus driver. The man was still wearing the shirt he'd died in, the stitching on the right breast pocket stating he had been an employee of the Transatlantic Bus Company. Henry noticed the corpse was missing its right hand.

Jimmy looked over Henry's shoulder at the corpse, and after noticing the missing hand, whispered into Henry's ear.

"Well, I guess that leaves one mystery solved. What do you say we get this guy outside and bunk down for the night?"

"Yeah, sure. Help me with him, will you?" Henry asked, reaching inside to grab a piece of the bus driver.

The corpse was nothing more than a hollow husk, the internal organs long dried; the skin resembling leather. The sides and floor of the stall were painted in a dark spray, the blood long dried to a dull brown color. Thankfully, the smell was minimal, and once the body was removed and the door was shut again, the odor was barely noticeable.

The two men carried the corpse outside and gently laid the man in the tall grass on the side of the highway guardrail. While Henry felt guilty for not giving the man a proper burial, when the dead were everywhere, walking around, trying to bury every corpse you'd find became overwhelming.

Instead, he had to settle for laying the body in the grass. That was enough dignity to give a stranger who had perished many months before.

Jimmy saw the hand in the dirt and gently kicked it across the grass so it came up against the body.

"Well, at least he's all together again," he said casually and walked over to the others.

After filling Mary, Cindy and Jeffrey in on what had occurred, the others boarded the bus. Everyone took a seat, and with Henry taking the first watch, the companions settled in for the night. While the bus wasn't as pleasant as the house they'd had to vacate, it was still better than a lot of the places they'd had to call home for a night or two over the past few months.

At least it was dry, he thought to himself, remembering the time they had to hold up in the sewers of a city while the undead prowled above them. They could have wandered around for days in the wet, filthy tunnels until coming across a manhole cover that was loose enough to pry open. He had remembered the sun had never looked so good that day.

Now, while the others relaxed and talked to themselves, Henry sat at the front of the bus in the driver's seat. The highway spread wide in front of him and for the hell of it he turned the key in the ignition where it had sat all these months.

Nothing.

Not even a soft click from the starter. The battery was as dead as the city they now found themselves in.

He knew it would be, of course, but had still hoped otherwise.

Maybe that was why he and his friends were still alive. Despite the condition of the United States, and for all he knew, the world, he still had hope, as did his friends.

Hope that there was a safe place out there in America where the undead weren't. A place in which he and his friends could live without the fear of being attacked at every turn. Whether from fellow human beings or the undead.

Henry daydreamed out the front windshield at all the possibilities the lonely road in front of him held for his friends and him.

Now all they had to do was find them.

CHAPTER TEN

THE SUN ROSE the next morning, the rays shining through the front windshield of the bus, blasting the companions with its brilliance. The group was already up and about. While each person made trips to the side of the bus to attend to nature's calling, Cindy and Mary prepared a light breakfast of canned beans and crackers.

"Now, don't get any ideas that the women are going to do this all the time, Henry. Those days are over," Mary joked while she set out the meal.

"Honey, I wouldn't even think it," Henry smiled, reaching down for an open can of beans.

At the moment, Jimmy was outside keeping watch as Jeffrey squatted in the tall grass.

"Hey, Jeffrey, watch out for snakes, they'll reach up and bite it right off," he joked.

Jeffrey frowned. "Very funny, but we both know that's not true. Besides, it's much too cold for a snake to survive in this environment." Still, the little man watched the grass a little more carefully.

Once everyone had attended to the body's necessities they all gathered in the bus. While the meal was consumed, Henry filled them in on the schedule for the day.

"I figure we'll walk another ten miles or so today, then we'll really need to find a place to hole up for the winter. I was thinking of a hotel or a factory."

"What about a school? They usually have reinforced windows and steel doors."

"That's a great idea, Jimmy," Mary said from behind him.

"Thanks, Mary," he said, feeling good about the compliment.

Mary smiled to herself. Men, just pat them on the head a few times and they act just like puppies.

When breakfast was finished, the companions gathered their belongings and started down the highway once again. The sun was bright, although the temperature had dropped a few degrees. The clouds floated by overhead, a few cumulous clouds peppering the sky with white spots like cotton balls.

Henry gazed at them as they floated past overhead. Did they look a little whiter than from weeks before?

Nah, probably just his imagination.

*   *   *

The miles went by under their feet, the companions slogging on. Once in a while a zombie could be seen off the side of the highway, but the Jersey barriers or fences kept them from coming near the five survivors.

Watching the ghouls warily, the group trudged on.

By mid-day everyone was feeling tired, leg muscles wanting a small respite, when the sound of an engine could be heard floating on the wind.

"You hear that?" Jimmy asked, looking around for any signs of the vehicle.

"Yeah, but where's it coming from?" Henry asked.

Mary was the first to spot the vehicle. Rising out of a dip in the road, a tow truck was heading directly for their group.

Before Henry could give orders for everyone to take cover, a bullet whined by his ear, so close he heard the wind as the round displaced the air by its passage. Luckily, it missed him, but by no more than an inch.

"Take cover, now!" He yelled, diving behind the shattered wreck of an old station wagon. Mary followed him and the others dove behind the burnt out wreck of a small compact car. The burnt husk of the driver was still strapped to the driver's seat, forever stuck in traffic.

The tow truck moved closer and stopped when it was no more than fifty yards away.

Henry waited for their visitors to make the first move.

"Hello! Anyone there!" A voice called to them. "We mean you no harm."

"Yeah, then why'd you shoot at us?" Henry called back. If there was a way to get out of this without a gunfight, then he was all for it.

"Yeah, sorry about that. That was young Timmy here. He gets a little itchy with the trigger. He thought you guys were rotters."

Henry looked at Mary. "Rotters? You think he means roamers?"

Mary shrugged. "Sure, why not, it's probably shorthand for deaders. Ask him."

Henry turned back to the vehicle idling in the middle of the highway.

"Did you think we were zombies?" He asked.

The man nodded. "Yup, 'fraid so. From a distance who could tell, besides it's not like we get a lot of visitors out here."

A moan sounded from Henry's side and he noticed a few roamers trying to get over the Jersey barriers. If he didn't decide what to do soon, the companions would have to deal with the truck's occupants as well as the undead.

"Cover me, Mary. If any of them makes a wrong move, light 'em up," Henry said, moving to the front of the station wagon.

She nodded and raised her weapon a little higher.

"All right, I'm coming out to talk, but my friends are armed. Any sudden…"

The man in the truck cut him off. "Yeah, yeah, I know the drill. Any sudden moves and we'll blast ya. I get it."

The man jumped down off the back of the tow truck and walked to the halfway point between the two groups. Henry did the same. His Glock was in his hand, but he kept it aimed to the ground. But the message was clear.

Fuck with him and get a bullet in the head.

The two men met in the middle of the highway. Henry was already summing up the man in front of him, trying to get a feel for him.

The man had a deep brown beard that covered the bottom portion of his face. His clothes were worn, but clean, the boots looking like they'd seen better days.

The man held a hunting rifle, a .22 if Henry was accurate, in his left hand; the weapon swinging by his side.

It was the man's eyes that Henry noticed next. Although the man was smiling, his eyes showed none of it, the blue orbs like ice.

He held out his hand for Henry to take.

"Hey, name's Keith. Keith Conrad."

Henry looked at the hand in front of him, as if he was pondering his next move. Then with a slight shrug, he holstered his Glock, and reached out to shake the man's hand. The firm grasp was strong, but not strong enough the man was playing games. They both released their grip and stood watching each other.

"Names Henry Watson."

"So, how many you got back there behind those cars?" Keith asked.

"Enough. What do you want? You should know we're well armed," Henry said, his voice level.

Keith looked down at the Glock on Henry's hip. "I can see that. Got you some firepower, too."

Henry nodded, letting the other man do the talking. More ghouls had been arriving, attracted to the noise of the tow truck's engine.

"Hey, Keith, we got company," one of the men in the back of the tow truck called.

Henry had already deduced there were four men; two in the cab and one on the back; plus Keith.

Keith looked around the area and saw the zombies trying to climb the barriers.

"Shit, more rotters. Look, friend, that stray shot was really an accident. If you want, you can come back with us. We've got ourselves setup pretty good in a shopping mall not too far from here. Plenty of food and power."

Henry's eyes went up a little. "Oh yeah? And what if we don't want to come?"

Keith shrugged. "Shit, man, it's all the same to me. Stay here and play with the rotters if you want."

Jimmy's voice floated over to Henry. "What are we gonna do, Chief? I really don't feel like wasting ammo today," he said, watching the undead getting closer.

Henry looked behind him to Mary, his eyes asking her opinion.

She smiled and nodded. "What do we have to lose?" She called.

Henry agreed. They didn't have that much to lose if they stayed. Just more miles to walk and an uncertain future of where they'd end up. This could just be the break they'd been looking for.

"We keep our weapons. I give you my word we won't use them unless provoked."

Keith nodded. "Fair enough, besides, the whole enclave is armed, anyway."

A moan sounded from the side of the highway as three corpses shambled into view.

Keith turned to his men, one standing in the road and the other on the back of the truck. "Take those rotting fucks out!" He yelled. Then he looked at Henry to make sure the man was okay with it.

He was. Let them waste their own ammo on the walking corpses.

The two men by the truck raised their rifles and in no time the undead were dead for good. Maggots could be seen squirming around in the open head wounds, the stench of the bodies carrying to the companions on the air currents.

Henry started to breathe through his mouth as the wind blew the odor into his face.

Keith waved his hand in front of his face, as well. "Damn, those bastards smell. Well, come on if you're comin'. My boys don't need target practice today."

Henry nodded and turned to his friends and waved them on.

"Come on, it seems safe enough. Just watch your back."

Henry turned to see Keith smiling. "Good advice, my friend, no matter where you are. Come on, we'll do introductions later when we're safe."

Two minutes later, the companions were hanging onto the back of the tow truck with Keith and Timmy next to them.

As the truck pulled around the station wagon, Jimmy noticed a couple of large cloth bags about six feet long and two feet wide lying on the bed of the tow truck in front of the winch.

"What's in there?" Jimmy asked Keith.

The bearded man looked down, saw what Jimmy was pointing to and just waved the question away.

"Nothing that matters, just some supplies for the enclave."

Then the man looked forward again as if the question was answered.

The truck headed down the road, the now ten ghouls left standing in the sun on the highway, their meal slowly getting away.

Not knowing what to do, they started up the highway, following in the wake of the tow truck, their rotting legs moving them forward, one step at a time.

CHAPTER ELEVEN

FIFTEEN MINUTES LATER, the tow truck pulled off the main highway, the vehicle swerving around a few derelict cars.

The truck drove down a side street until it pulled off into a wide open parking lot.

In front of the truck was a shopping mall. A giant sign sat on top of one part of the massive building, claiming: THE CRYSTAL MALL, One Stop Shopping For All Your Needs. Henry noticed the S in Crystal had fallen off the building and was now lying on the concrete, the undead now walking over it.

Henry noticed the first of two things as the tow truck drove closer to the shopping mall. The first was the amount of the undead that were surrounding the building, the second was how fortified the openings to the mall were.

From Henry's vantage point, he was only able to see one side of the massive two-story building, but the entrances into the mall seemed well secure.

Large, chain-link fences were doubled, one over the other, and had then been welded to the metal frame of the building. Thus, the undead could pull and push all they wanted, but without manmade tools, they would never gain entry.

The tow truck drove wide in the parking area, easily avoiding crowds of the undead as they wandered around aimlessly.

Keith noticed Henry watching everything and smiled.

"Bet your wondering how we're gonna get inside, huh?" The bearded man asked.

Henry nodded. "Well, yeah, it did cross my mind. I have to admit, I'm curious. How the hell do you manage it without having to fight off a boat load of the dead every time?"

Keith pulled a shortwave radio from his pocket.

"Watch and learn, my new friend," he said, and then spoke into the radio.

"Home base this is Scout 1, we're outside. Start the pinger."

"Ten-four, just give me a second Keith," a voice said from the radio's speaker.

"Well, make it quick, they're getting riled up out here and I don't feel like being the main course," Keith snapped.

Then Henry heard it, a pinging sound, like what a submarine would use for sonar; except this was loud enough to shake the glass in the truck. No sooner had the sound started than almost all of the zombies started to wander away across the parking lot. As soon as the building was clear of the undead, the truck's driver floored the gas pedal and the tow truck shot across the pavement to the loading docks of the shopping mall.

The bay doors were raised and the truck drove inside. As soon as the truck was in, the doors slammed shut, blocking out the pinging to the point it was nothing more than an afterthought. A few stray ghouls wandered in, evidently more interested in the loading dock than the pinger and were quickly dispatched by guards with rifles similar to Keith's.

Keith jumped down from the truck and called into the radio again.

"We're inside, Mickey. Turn it off."

A muffled, "okay" could be heard before Keith pushed the radio back into his coat.

The companions had hopped down to the floor of the loading dock and were standing around waiting.

Henry walked over to Mary and whispered into her ear.

"Stay sharp, I still don't trust any of these guys yet. When you get a chance, make sure you tell the others that no one goes anywhere alone."

Mary nodded and slowly moved next to Cindy to pass on what she'd been told at the first opportunity.

Keith was talking to a couple of men at the top of the docks, pointing to the prone corpses, and as soon as he was finished, he walked back to the companions.

"I've called Barry and he's looking forward to meeting you," Keith said, ushering them out of the loading bays.

As the companions followed, Jimmy spoke up.

"Who's Barry?" He asked.

From the front of the line, Keith called back to Jimmy, although he knew all the companions could hear him.

"Barry is quite simply put, our savior. He was the man who figured out that we could hold up here. He was the manager of the mall before the rains came and when everything went to hell, he had the vision to start barricading this place up.

Then he let anyone who arrived in, until he was at the perfect number."

"And what is that number, exactly?" Mary asked while they walked.

"Six-hundred and fifty. To the person," Keith answered.

"And where does that leave us?" Henry asked.

Keith turned askance of Henry and smiled.

"Relax, Henry. I said we started at six-hundred and fifty. But since we've had to go out foraging, we've lost a few men here and there, so there's plenty of room for you and your friends."

The front of the line had reached a set of double doors. Keith pushed them open and the group walked out into the main hall of the mall.

The first thing Henry and the others noticed was the clear glass for the ceiling. This allowed the sun to illuminate the mall in the daytime as well as help to keep it warm in the winter. The second thing they noticed was how clean everything was.

The mall looked like any other day out of its past, with the exception of where the stores once were, now they were being used for dormitories for the people who called the mall home.

Looking up to the second floor, the stores were all being used for homes there as well.

"Impressive, you turned the mall into a giant hotel," Henry said as they walked along the hallway in the middle of the giant atrium.

As they walked, people would stop what they were doing and study the outsiders as they moved through the building. This was nothing new for the companions. No matter where they went, they were always scrutinized. It seemed with every new day less people were traveling across America.

Keith led them to the end of the mall and up an out of order escalator. It was immediately obvious they were in what was once the food court. The different vendor's signs still sat above the various openings in the walls of the large room. Inside most of the kitchens, women and a few men could be seen cooking. The companions couldn't see what was being cooked, but the smell of the spices being used to flavor the food was tantalizing. Thick clouds of smoke could be seen curling upwards to where an opening had been made in the ceiling to vent it.

"What are they cooking?" Jeffrey asked from the back of the line as they entered the food court.

"Actually they're smoking and curing meat, so we'll have enough for the winter."

"Oh yeah? What kind of meat?" Jimmy asked; his curiosity peaked.

Keith hesitated for a moment and then smiled.

"Mostly dog, a few deer and maybe some cat," he said, then quickly changed the subject. "Follow me. Barry wanted me to bring you to him as soon as we got back."

The companions followed Keith to the end of the food court. Keith opened a fire door and started up a set of cement steps. The companions followed, their footsteps echoing loudly. Upon reaching the top landing, they proceeded down another smaller hallway; the width only enough for two people to walk side by side. At reaching the end of this hallway, Keith directed them to another door set at the end.

"I'm not going with you. Just go through that door and you'll be in Barry's office. He's waiting for you and is looking forward to meeting you."

He started walking away. "Until later, guys."

The man's footsteps receded down the steps and disappeared with the sound of the fire door opening and closing again down below.

Henry stood at the front of the line, with his friend's faces looking back at him.

"Well," he said, "let's go meet Barry."

CHAPTER TWELVE

BARRY WAS THE framed picture of what a politician should look like.

The man was wearing a gray three-piece suit that seemed perfectly at home on his average-size frame. The man reminded Henry of every paper pusher he'd ever met.

Barry's receding hairline and chubby cheeks only added to the picture.

As the companions filed into the small office overlooking what was once the food court, the man stood up from behind his desk. Moving with a grace that bellied his looks, he walked around to the front of his desk and leaned against the right corner. Another overhead skylight bathed the room in the soft glow of the sun.

"Ah, at last. I've been so looking forward to meeting you all. We get so few visitors nowadays. I'm Barry Gomez," he said in a light Spanish accent while holding out his hand for Henry to shake.

Shaking the man's hand, Henry was impressed when Barry gripped his hand firmly. Pumping twice, he then let go and moved on to Jimmy. Once the greeting was over, Barry promptly turned to the two women in their group.

"Ah, what a picture of loveliness. I am so happy to make your acquaintances." Barry said, while cupping Mary's hand in both of his.

"Uh, hello," Mary said, not quite sure how to respond to the man's enthusiasm.

Barry let go of her hand and then quickly reached for Cindy's.

"And who is this vision of beauty?" Barry inquired, while doing the same to Cindy's hand as to Mary's.

"That's Cindy, my girlfriend," Jimmy said, moving between the two of them.

Barry looked up into Jimmy's face. The younger man had about three inches on the bureaucrat.

"Of course it is, my dear boy. I apologize if you thought anything untoward by my greeting. And who might you be?"

Henry spoke up, pointing at each of the companions in turn.

"I'm Henry Watson, that's Jimmy Cooper. Over there is Mary Roberts, and the blonde woman is Cindy Jansen and the little guy is Jeffrey Robbins."

"Little guy? Thanks a lot," Jeffrey said, his feelings hurt.

"Sorry, Jeffrey, it's the easiest description of you," Henry apologized.

"Wonderful, I'm so very glad to meet you all. It's always good news when we are adding to our numbers."

"What do you mean by that?" Jimmy asked, sitting down in one of the two seats in the office.

"Why, the obvious of course. You five do plan on staying with us for good don't you?"

"We're not sure," Henry said. "We kind of like to move around."

"Really, out there? With all those distasteful dead things running around?" Barry said, surprised.

"Yeah, well, we know how to handle ourselves," Jimmy said from his chair. One of the springs had broken and was even now poking his left butt cheek.

"I see, from the look of your armaments, I suppose you do," Barry said, moving back around his desk and sitting dropping into his chair.

"But if the offer is open, we'd like to stay the winter. We can do whatever's needed to contribute," Henry asked politely.

Barry seemed to think about it for a second and then his face lit up in a smile.

"I don't see why not. You three men should be an excellent compliment to the foraging teams and we can always use a few more women in the kitchen or laundry."

"Kitchen? Laundry? Now wait just a damn sec…" Mary started to say until Henry spoke over her.

"That sounds great; we also have a lot of our own supplies. We came across a house that hadn't been looted yet," Henry said quickly, glaring at Mary to keep quiet.

"Really, my, that was fortunate. Over the past few months we've had to patrol farther away to find food. Luckily, we've started some alternative forms of nourishment to keep the camp fed."

"Oh, really, may I ask what they are?" Jeffrey asked from the corner of the room.

"Not now, later, my friend. For now why don't you get something to eat and we'll assign you some living quarters. If its one thing we have, it's plenty of space," Barry beamed; proud of his creation. "Once you're settled in, why don't you five join me for dinner. I'll have someone retrieve you. Say six o'clock?"

Henry looked at his wrist watch. It was just going on four o' clock. They had two hours to get settled and get the lay of the land, so to speak.

"That'll be fine," Henry told Barry and turned to open the office door.

But upon opening the door, Henry stopped suddenly.

Keith and two more men were waiting in the hallway. By the way they stood and the rifles over their shoulders, it was fairly obvious they were some sort of security force for the mall.

Barry saw past Henry and waved Keith inside the room.

"Ah, Keith, excellent. I was just about to send for you. Please see these people receive a place of berth, as well as a brief tour of our little enclave."

Keith nodded and pointed to the two guards. "You two, take care of it. Bring them to the north side, by the toy store. There's plenty of room there."

"Yes, sir," the first guard said, while the other one just nodded yes.

"If you'll follow me, please?" The first guard said to Henry and the others. Henry followed the man with the rest of the companions following behind. Barry gave smiles all around as the companions left, waving with his right hand.

"Goodbye, friends, I'll see you at dinner. Then we'll talk of your travels. I'm looking forward to it."

When Jeffrey was the last one to exit the room, the second guard fell in step behind the small man.

Keith closed the door to the office, leaving himself alone in the room with Barry.

The second the door closed, though, the smile on Barry's face disappeared, to be replaced with a look of distaste.

"Why the fuck did you bring them back here? You should have disposed of them on the road!" Barry snapped, his right hand slapping the desk in anger, causing a cup of pencils to jump an inch into the air and fall to the floor. They were ignored.

"But Boss, you saw their hardware. It was just me and Timmy and two others. We would've been slaughtered. I figured I'd bring them back and let them get comfortable. Once their guard is down, it should be child's play to take them out."

Barry mulled Keith's statement over for a few seconds, his teeth worrying the inside of his cheek. Keith always got a kick out of this. It made Barry look like he was a fish, although he'd never say so to the man's face.

"Perhaps you're right. It could actually prove even more beneficial. They'd be fresher that way."

"Exactly, that's what I thought," Keith said, breathing a sigh of relief.

Barry looked up at his security chief and smiled. "Bullshit, you did not think of that, but fine, we'll do it your way. But if you screw this up, it'll be you taking their place."

Keith swallowed hard, not foreseeing that fly in the ointment.

"Not to worry, Boss, I won't disappoint you."

"See that you don't, now leave me. I have a lot of paperwork to do before dinner."

Keith stood up and walked out of the room. Glancing over his shoulder, he saw Barry was already busy writing in folders and notebooks.

That always freaked out the security chief. The world of paperwork and nine to five jobs was over. So then what the hell was Barry doing?

Secretly, Keith had a feeling his superior was cracking up with the strain of trying to keep them all alive. After all, he couldn't imagine what it felt like to have over five-hundred people depending on every decision you made to keep them alive.

Closing the office door behind him, Keith headed down the hallway. There was a lot of work to do before dinner and he knew it would be his hide if it wasn't completed in time.

CHAPTER THIRTEEN

HENRY AND THE others followed the lead security guard down the wide spacious hallways of the mall, their footsteps echoing off the polished walls.

All around them, the hustle and bustle of everyday life continued.

Mothers fed and washed their children's faces, old timers played checkers or chess or young couples made love behind hastily draped sheets for privacy.

A group of young children ran by the companions, making Mary pause and smile.

"You have children here," she stated to the guard.

The guard nodded. "Sure do. All together I think we have about thirty kids. We've setup a school and everything."

"Really, where does that happen?" Mary asked.

"They took over one of the stores and made it into a classroom. Misses Willis teaches them. Before all the shit happened out there, she was a second grade teacher," the guard said, waving to the walls, signifying the world surrounding the mall.

Mary smiled. "How nice."

Seemed the guard was in a talking mood, Henry took advantage. "What's that pinging thing we heard when we came in here today?"

"Oh that? One of our residents was an engineer. He jury rigged something to a couple of bass speakers. Whenever it's on, the rotters go to it like it's a dinner bell.

"Shit, that's pretty clever. They can clear the bay doors whenever they want to leave," Jimmy commented.

A pretty girl walked by wearing a tight pair of jeans and a shirt that showed off her midriff. Jimmy followed her with his eyes until Cindy nudged him in the ribs, the gesture hard enough to cause him to grunt.

With a slight chuckle, he turned to her and smiled. "Sorry, babe, old habits and all that."

Cindy simply frowned and crossed her arms in front of her.

The guard at the back of the line had been waiting while his coworker kept gabbing and so he finally spoke up.

"All right, Ted, that's enough talking. I'm sure Barry will tell them whatever they need to know later. Let's go, I've got Rosie waiting on me and I don't like to keep her waiting."

The first guard smiled and leaned a little closer to Henry. "Rosie's his girlfriend, although she acts more like his wife," he joked.

Henry nodded, amused. The guard started forward again and the companions followed. All eyes were on them, the residents curious as to whom the new arrivals were.

Turning a corner, the guard started down a stationary escalator, different from the last one the companions had been on, the boots of the group clanging on the metal stairs as they moved to the bottom.

The guard pointed to the end of the long, wide hallway.

"That's where you can bunk down for the time being. We've got more than enough room."

Henry nodded and the companions moved down the hall. The stores on both sides of the hallway were empty, the merchandise long used or scavenged. Large white sheets hung in front of some of the openings, proclaiming these places were already in use. Most still had the glass doors that separated them from the hallway, though, and one of these was what Henry steered the guard to. At least with the doors, they'd have some form of a barrier from the rest of the community.

It wasn't much, but it was better than nothing.

"We'll take that one," Henry said, pointing to a store that had once sold items for a dollar. The first guard looked at the second guard, his eyes asking if it was okay. Guard number two just shrugged. "Sure whatever, it's all the same to me."

The first guard moved to walk away, but paused for a second. Looking at Henry, he said loud enough for the other companions to hear.

"Stay here until dinner, don't go wandering around. At least not until you know the rules. Wouldn't want you getting hurt or anything like that."

Jimmy was about to put his foot in his mouth when Henry spoke up, quickly.

"Sure, no problem, we'll be here. Wouldn't want to make any waves."

The second guard snorted and walked away. The first guard nodded and followed his friend, the two guards moving down the hallway side by side.

When the companions were finally alone in their new living quarters, they gathered in a circle, careful to make sure they weren't overheard, despite the fact they should be alone.

"So what do you think?" Henry asked the others.

"I don't like it, there's something off about that Barry guy," Jimmy said quietly.

"Oh, please, that's what you always say," Jeffrey spoke up. "I think we wandered into a good thing here. If we play our cards right, we could spend the whole winter here."

Jimmy was about to reply when Mary spoke up, quickly. The last thing she wanted was to listen to the two of them bickering about something trivial.

"I have to agree with Jeffrey. The people seem nice and they have plenty of food and water and seem to be safe in here. Maybe we should stay here for the winter, hell, maybe for good."

Henry thought about it. "It would be nice to take a break for a while. All right, why don't we see how it goes, but stay sharp. We've been places before that aren't what they seem to be and I'll be damned if I'm gonna get caught with my pants down again."

One such instance Henry was referring to occurred not more than a month ago. They had holed up with a group of about fifteen men. The men had barricaded an old welding shop on the outskirts of the town. They had constructed a metal bridge that spanned the roof from their building to the ones next door, thus allowing them to sneak in and out undetected by the undead. When Henry and the others had met them, the men had greeted them with open arms. At least until their real motives came out.

They had planned to kill Henry, Jimmy and Jeffrey and were then going to keep Mary and Cindy for themselves. With a little luck, and a whole lot of bullets, the companions had made it out of there in one piece. Henry still remembered as a parting gift, he had unlocked the front doors to the welding shop, allowing the walking corpses to flood into the building. He had never got the chance to hear the men's screams, but he could imagine what they sounded like when they turned the corner in the building looking for the companions and had walked into a horde of the undead. Justice may have disappeared with the fall of humanity, but vengeance was still alive and well.

Everyone nodded agreement and the group separated. The women and Jeffrey went to the far corners of their temporary home to inspect the inside while Jimmy and Henry stepped into the hallway and walked over to the glass railing that looked down on the floor below.

People were moving about on the errands of living and surviving and Henry turned to Jimmy.

"You know, if this place does work out, then we might have finally found a home."

Jimmy nodded, "Sure, would be nice. Can't say I wouldn't mind sleeping in the same bed for more than a few times for a change," he said.

Henry continued watching the people below him as they in turn did the same.

Then a group of children walked by with a couple of adults for chaperones.

From the back of her head, the woman at the front of the line looked like a double for his wife Emily, but he knew that was impossible. His wife was still lying in their kitchen with her head smashed in.

Still, he felt the unfamiliar feeling of butterflies in his stomach.

Almost as if the woman knew she was being watched, she turned her head and looked up at the two men above her. Henry saw a middle-aged woman of no more than forty with clear skin and a beautiful smile.

She wasn't Emily, but she was still beautiful.

A man was walking by them and Henry turned and asked the man a question.

"Excuse me, who's that woman down there?" The man looked over the side and then back to Henry.

"Oh, that's Miss Willis; she's the schoolteacher around here, why?" The man asked.

"No reason, just thought I knew her, that's all. Thanks for your help."

The man smiled and continued on. Jimmy saw Henry watching the woman as she walked away and he smirked.

"Henry's got a girlfriend," he joked.

Henry came out of his daze and looked at Jimmy. "What did you say?"

Jimmy smiled a little wider. "I said, I know that look, hell, I get it all the time, at least until I met Cindy. You like her, don't you?"

"Like her, I don't even know her," Henry said, brushing away Jimmy's assumptions.

"Say what you want," Jimmy said, while he pushed off the railing to join the others in their bunks. "But I know that look. You've just been bitten by the love bug."

Then, before Henry could reply, he jogged across the hallway and disappeared into the store.

Henry stood at the railing, thinking.

For just a moment that woman had reminded him of his wife. And when she had turned, he still hadn't been disappointed. Maybe Jimmy was right, maybe he was attracted to her… she was pretty.

Letting out a pent up sigh, he stepped away from the railing. As he moved closer to the store, he could already hear Jimmy and Jeffrey arguing about something. Shaking his head like a father who's disappointed in his two sons, Henry stepped into the store, prepared to break up yet another disagreement.

CHAPTER FOURTEEN

THE GROUP PASSED the ninety minutes getting situated in their new surroundings. While they were allowed to stay armed it would have just been overkill to walk around with their shotguns and Cindy's rifle, so Henry got the bright idea to hide them in the rafters, up behind the ceiling panels.

Henry kept his Glock and placed the .357 S&W in the back waistband of his pants, the loose bottom of his shirt helping to hide the bulge. While this wasn't the optimum place to keep it, he felt it better to have the weapon more easily accessible in exchange for comfort. Both Jimmy and Mary had their .38s, but Jeffrey was still unarmed. Henry told him when they had a chance, he'd see about finding the man a .22 or something of equally small caliber. Something the man could handle without shooting himself by accident.

Their gear was placed in the corner of the room with the empty shelves protecting them from view. Before they left, Henry placed a few strands of thread from his shirt over the zippers to the packs.

Jeffrey noticed this and walked over to stand behind him.

"What are you doing?" The little man asked.

"I'm laying some thread over the zippers, that way if anyone gets nosy, at least we'll know about it. Besides, all the really valuable stuff like ammo and the shotguns are hidden, so it's not like they'd get anything of much use."

"You really think that'll happen here, while we're gone for dinner?" Jeffrey asked.

Henry shrugged his wide shoulders. "Don't know, but if it does, I want to know about it."

Mary walked to the back and interrupted the two men.

"A guard's here. Says he's here to take us to dinner," Mary said and then disappeared back out front.

"Well, you heard the lady, shall we go dine?" Henry asked Jeffrey.

Jeffrey smiled. "Yeah, I guess we will."

Then the two men walked out front to join the others, the packs forgotten for now.

*   *   *

Torches lit with kerosene illuminated the now darkened mall, the sun having left the sky more than an hour ago.

The walk through the mall went quick and a little less than ten minutes later, the companions had returned to the food court. In the corner of the large open room sat a group of tables that had been pushed together to form a mock replica of a grander, larger table. Table clothes librated from one of the stores covered the table tops, completing the look of one large piece of furniture.

Office dividers stood around the outside of the massive table and chairs, lending a small amount of privacy from the rest of the food court. It was there, at the head of the table, that the companions met Barry for the second time that day.

Torches lined the outside of the dining area and a few candles were sprinkled in with the glasses and plates covering the table. The area surrounding them was a flutter of activity as the residents ate their meals.

At the companion's arrival, Barry stood up and clapped his hands.

"Ah, excellent, right on time. Please sit down and we'll start dinner. I don't know about you, but I'm famished."

The group sat down with Henry sitting next to Barry and Jimmy on the other side.

Cindy sat next to Jimmy and Mary took the seat next to Henry.

Jeffrey, being the odd man out, sat at the end of the table, directly across from Barry and the rest of the table had a few guards and miscellaneous people.

Barry rang a small bell sitting on the table in front of him and within moments two women wearing dirty white aprons started pushing out small, wheeled serving tables with steaming bowls of food on them.

"I hope you all like this; it's a specialty of our cooks. As I said, we've had to make do with whatever we could find out there when the pickings began to grow slim."

The group looked down at the brown stew sitting in their bowls. Henry used his spoon to move around a piece of the unidentifiable meat.

He marveled at how no matter where they seemed to wind up, stew was usually on the menu. But then again, when you had a bunch of odds and ends from salvaged canned goods, stew usually was the most practical use for the products. It was a great way to stretch limited resources.

Jeffrey was the first to dig in, and with a slice of homemade bread that had been placed on the table in front of him, was eagerly devouring his meal.

Barry noticed this and smiled. "How is your meal, my friend?"

Jeffrey chewed what was in his mouth and swallowed. "Not bad; what kind of meat is it? It's kind of gamey."

"I believe its dog or perhaps squirrel. I'm really not sure. I'd have to ask the cook."

"It's not squirrel. I've had squirrel before," Jimmy said while taking another bite. "Not bad though."

"Good, I'm glad you all like it," the man said while taking a healthy spoonful of his own stew and shoveling it into his mouth. Then he changed the subject.

"So, if you are now part of our little community, I would like you to join one of my foraging teams tomorrow morning."

Henry shrugged, pausing while he chewed a piece of meat slowly.

"Sure, Barry, that's fine. We'll pull our own weight around here."

"Excellent. And the women can work in the laundry or perhaps help with keeping the mall clean. While every resident does his share over their respective areas, we still need people to sweep the common areas and the like."

"What do you people do about bathrooms, cause man I've got to go," Jimmy said as he placed his spoon down. Once he started eating, the machine of his body started to work overtime and now he needed to go bad.

Barry pointed to the bathroom area across the room where the doors marked men and women were located.

"Over there, my boy. After you go, use the buckets of water against the wall to fill the tank and then flush as usual. The water may not flow, but the sewers seem to still be in working condition."

Jimmy nodded and then ran off to attend to business.

Mary smiled as she watched him canter away. "Our Jimmy, such a gentlemen."

Keith walked up and sat down at the end of the table next to Jeffrey. Barry rang the bell again, and a second later, one of the women with a dirty apron rushed out with a bowl of stew. After placing it in front of Keith, the man dug in with gusto, shoveling the stew into his mouth as if he hadn't eaten for days.

"Ah, good, Keith," Barry said. "Our friends have decided to join you tomorrow on your foray into the new world."

Keith just nodded. "Okay, it's cool with me."

Cindy was eating quietly, watching everything, while Mary sat across from her. So far the conversation was just for the men.

What was this, the 1800s? She thought to herself.

Jeffrey was involved in his meal and had no interest in the goings on around him.

Henry had finished his meal and had sat back in his chair. Figuring he'd try to make some conversation, he asked Barry a few questions.

"So, Barry, how'd you end up here? How'd you manage to secure this place without getting torn apart by all the walking dead?"

Barry's eyes lit up. "Ah, now that is a tale worth telling," he said, placing his fork down and sitting back in his chair.

"I was the general manager of this mall before the rains came and turned most of the surrounding city into undead creatures. I saw how everything was falling apart and so chose to hold up here one day. I decided not to open the mall that day and when some of the store employees showed up, I suggested that they grab what they could from their homes and then to return here. Some did, but others chose not to. I still wonder what has happened to them, although I can probably surmise from the state of affairs in the surrounding town and of course the world." He scratched his nose with his left hand, then continued.

"But I digress. So once a large group of us was in here, we started to organize. We found that we had an engineer, a welder, a cook and a software engineer. As well as the usual clerks and cashiers. With the engineer and the welder's help, we were able to build the chain-link gates that cover the glass doors surrounding the building and then later, built the pinger."

Jimmy had returned, and with a more relaxed look on his face, sat back down.

"I hope you washed your hands," Mary joked from across the table.

Jimmy held up his hands. "Yup. See, they're still wet."

Barry looked at the young man and Jimmy realized he'd interrupted something. With downcast eyes, he apologized. "Oh, sorry dude, my bad."

Barry nodded, placated. "That's okay, my good man, I was nearly done anyway.

The pinger is a simple sound device that sends an electronic impulse through the ground and surrounding air. The rotters go nuts for it and head for it every time. Not like the old days when we had to drive around the parking lot and draw the rotters away from the doors so we could connect the chain-link fences and when we had to leave the loading dock." He looked at his watch and smiled. "Well, my friends, it's getting late, why don't we end this meal for the night and let you get some much needed rest."

Henry yawned. "That sounds like a great idea. I know I'm beat. It's been a long day."

"Amen to that," Jimmy said and the others agreed.

Barry stood up. "Well, then, until tomorrow. Sleep well."

Henry shook hands with the man again and then the companions followed another guard back to their place of berth.

Once they were in the general vicinity, Henry waved the guard away.

"Thanks, pal. We've got it from here," Henry said, stopping the man from walking closer to their sleeping quarters.

The guard nodded and moved away, but Henry noticed he stopped at the end of the hall where it forked off to the left and right. Was he there to keep an eye on them?

Probably, if he'd been in charge, he would have placed a guard to watch them, too.

The group entered their alcove and Henry went to the back to check their packs. Sure enough, the threads were missing. He quickly went through his gear and was surprised to find everything there. And the items were almost in the perfect order they had been packed in. If he hadn't known to look for signs of intrusion, he probably wouldn't have noticed anything was amiss.

Smiling to himself, he repacked his goods and prepared himself for the night; the others doing the same.

*　　*　　*

Back in a corner of the food court, out of hearing distance of the other diners, Barry and Keith were discussing tactics.

"I want you to take them out when they're sleeping tonight. Wait until around three in the morning. They say that's the best time to attack someone. Take a few of your best men, but whatever you do, keep it down. The residents have no idea what's going on and I want it to stay that way. Use knives, that should be best. Once you're done, you know what to do with the bodies."

Keith nodded, his bearded face hard. "No problem, Boss, I'll take care of it. You can count on me." Then he rose from his chair and walked away. Turning a corner, he was lost from sight.

Barry leaned back in his chair and smiled to himself. The outsiders should have been killed out on the road, but mistakes could be fixed.

Oh yes, a sharpened blade could fix many problems.

CHAPTER FIFTEEN

THE MALL WAS quiet, with the exception of some distant snoring floating up from the second floor. The torches were extinguished, the hallways of the mall only illuminated by the wan glow filtering through the skylights from the few stars that weren't playing hide and seek with the overhead clouds.

Down the hall from where the companions were sleeping, Keith and two others slipped in the shadows between storefronts. They all had sneakers on and wore no loose items. The three man assassin squad was doing their best to remain silent.

When they were no more than fifteen feet away, Keith held up his hand in the shadowy gloom.

"You two stay here. I want to scout ahead. Once I know it's safe, then I'll come back and get you. Then we'll cut the fucker's throats from ear to ear. But try not to kill the women. There's other uses for them."

The two guards nodded and smiled, the ambient light in the hallway reflecting off their teeth, their breathing growing harder with anticipation of what was to come. The two men Keith had chosen were coldhearts in their own right. That's why Keith kept them around. Sometimes people just needed to disappear, and these two men always did it well. If they enjoyed their work, well, that was fine with Keith.

Barry had his own man to do his dirty-work, but Vinnie was busy elsewhere in the mall. That was fine with Keith, too. He and the large Italian were always butting heads as to who was the true second in command in the mall.

Moving off from the two men, Keith slipped further down the hall. He was no more than two feet from the glass doors that would lead him into the companion's alcove.

Opening the left glass door, he slipped inside.

The sound of snoring could be heard from somewhere in the back of the room.

In the darkness, Keith smiled.

Good, they were sleeping soundly. They would never know what hit them.

He was about to open the glass door and leave to fetch his felloe assassins when he heard the sound of a revolver cocking. Turning fast, he peered into the darkness. Although it was dark, the features of a man could just be discerned.

Henry walked a little closer to Keith and jammed the .357 under his chin, the muzzle lost in the man's unkempt beard.

"Can I help you?" He whispered in the dark.

Keith stammered for a moment, totally taken off guard.

They had posted a watch!

That had never happened before. Usually the guests would sleep soundly, secure in the fact they had been welcomed into the enclave. At least on those few, rare occasions that the people had made it as far as the inside of the mall alive.

"No, I'm fine. Just wanted to make sure you folks were okay, that's all," Keith gasped out, the barrel of the gun cold against his neck.

"Oh really," Henry hissed. "And do you always do this at three in the morning?"

Before Keith could answer, Henry pressed the gun closer into his neck. He did it so hard there would still be a round mark on the man's neck come morning.

"Let's cut the bullshit, shall we? I don't know what you had planned, but if it wasn't for the fact that my friends need their beauty sleep, I'd blow your goddamn head off right now. You read me?"

Keith nodded emphatically, the sweat breaking out on his brow starting to fall across his eyes.

"Good, now I'll tell you what," Henry hissed. " I'm gonna forget this happened tonight and tomorrow we'll start fresh. All right?"

Keith nodded some more. "Yeah, sure, okay."

"Good, now get the hell out of here and don't come back."

Henry took the gun away from the man's neck, but still had it pointed at Keith's chest. Keith breathed a sigh of relief when the gun was removed from his throat, and with a large swallow of the saliva he'd accumulated in his mouth, he backed out of the store and crept down the hallway.

Once he'd reached the other two assassins, they bombarded him with questions.

"Well, are we going?" One asked.

"Are they sleeping?" Asked the other.

"Both of you, shut the fuck up," Keith hissed. "Forget it, the op is off. We'll do it another time."

The men were about to argue when Keith hissed again.

"I said no, dammit. Now, let's get the hell out of here," he hissed, but in a whisper, his voice barely carrying past the three men.

Giving up, the two men turned and crept back down the hallway, with Keith behind them.

Keith stopped and looked back at the glass doors in the darkened hall.

Tomorrow, he thought. It'll just have to happen tomorrow.

Wouldn't it be a shame if a stray bullet took out Henry and Jimmy while they were dealing with a pack of rotters? The women would never suspect fowl play, then either.

Feeling better about the coming day, and doing his best to put the shame of the night-creep behind him, Keith smiled in the darkness.

Tomorrow, he would set things right and vindicate himself with Barry.

Tomorrow, he would kill the outsiders.

*   *   *

In the companion's alcove, Mary woke from a fitful dream.

Standing up, she noticed a shadowy figure over by the front doors. Moving closer, she relaxed when she saw the distinctive outline of Henry's head and shoulders.

"What are you still doing up?" She asked while yawning.

"Huh? Oh, I couldn't sleep, thought I'd stand watch."

"Really? In here? Don't you think we're safe?"

He smiled in the dark. "Of course we're safe, but it never hurts to be cautious."

She nodded, still groggy from sleep. He noticed and gave her a gentle push back to bed.

"Go on, go back to sleep. Tomorrow's gonna be fun. First day in the laundry room and all that."

She frowned. "Yuck, don't remind me." Yawning again, she headed back to bed.

With a soft wave, she left him. "Don't stay up too long."

"I won't, night," he whispered.

A muffled: "Night," came back to him.

"Will you people shut the fuck up? Some of us want to sleep back here," Jimmy's annoyed voice floated to the front of the room.

"Sorry, Jimmy; go back to bed, we'll be quiet," Henry assured the younger man.

"Good, thank you," Jimmy replied back, then turned over and went back to sleep with Cindy curled up next to him. She had taken all the covers and he yanked some over to his side. What was it about women and the bedcovers?

Then the silence reigned again.

Except for Jeffrey's snoring, of course.

Chapter Sixteen

"Okay, start the pinger," Keith said over the two-way radio.

Static filled the speaker and then a faint, "10-4," was heard.

Thirty seconds later, the faint sound of the thumping permeated the bay doors of the loading dock.

Keith looked over at Jimmy and Henry. "Now, all we have to do is wait a few minutes until our spotter on the roof tells us the rotters have all moved away from the doors. Works every time."

"Hope you're right, if not, then we're in for a world of shit when you open those doors," Henry stated.

"I bet my life on it," Keith added.

"That's good, because if you're wrong, that's the first thing your gonna lose," Jimmy said.

Keith looked at Jimmy for a second longer than he needed, but the meaning was clear. Henry had filled Jimmy in on what had happened the night before and now both men knew to watch their backs while on the supply run. Whatever was Keith's game, he'd lost the element of surprise by underestimating Henry and the others. Mary and Cindy had also been informed to watch their backs.

Besides Henry and Jimmy, Keith had three others with him. Two had the looks of men who knew to handle themselves, but the third was barely out of high school. The kid held a .22 rifle in his hands and his countenance told a tale of fear. Henry decided to see how the kid was doing while they waited to leave.

"Hey, son, what's your name?" Henry asked.

"Mark, sir, Mark Eckles."

"Well, Mark, relax. The best way to come back in one piece is to keep your head out there. Remember, those things out there aren't human anymore, don't hesitate to take one out if it threatens you. And always keep moving. You're faster than them, use that to your advantage." Then Henry slapped the kid on the back. "Don't worry, you'll be fine."

Mark nodded and seemed to calm down a little. Jimmy watched Henry and the kid. It reminded him of just six months ago when everything had gone to Hell. He had been as naïve as that kid back then.

The six men sat in the bed of a Ford F-150. The trucks tires had been modified to cover harsh terrain. Jimmy wondered if Ford had thought about the zombie apocalypse when it was making its pickup trucks. He could see the commercials now. "Built Ford tough, when zombies got you down, get a Ford truck. Number one with all survivors ages twenty to forty." And then they'd show the truck running down zombies and crushing them under the massive wheels. Why they'd sell millions. Hell he'd buy one.

Henry noticed Jimmy smiling to himself and Henry's eyebrows went up with curiosity. Jimmy just shook his head.

"It's nothing, just thought of something, not even worth mentioning."

Henry nodded and was then distracted by the crackling radio in Keith's hand.

"All set to go, Keith, the doors are clear, over," the disembodied voice said from the speaker.

Keith set his jaw. "All right then. You two in the front, the rest of us will stay in back and pick off the ones that get too close."

The two hard-asses jumped off the back and climbed into the cab, then, with the revving of the powerful engine, the driver got ready to leave while the bay doors started to slowly open.

Henry looked at Jimmy and grimaced. "You ready for this?"

"Am I ever?" Jimmy replied and then the truck shot out of the loading dock and into the morning sunlight.

* * *

The truck swerved in and around the wrecks on the road, some with the occupants still rotting in the seats. Many had blood splattered windows and doors, illustrating the carnage that had come before at the beginning of the outbreak.

It was a crisp morning, the temperature being in the mid-forties.

Sitting in the bed of the truck, the wind made it seem even colder and Henry closed the front on his new coat.

All the companions wore new clothes. Barry had let them take what they wanted from the shelves of a Marshalls department store that was closed for business for the foreseeable future. It was amazing what a clean pair of socks and a new shirt could do for your disposition.

The truck sideswiped a plodding ghoul in the road, its ankle snapping under the front tire of the large truck. The sound, like a twig breaking, floated up and away as the truck barreled down the road.

"Does he always drive like this?" Henry asked, holding on as the truck bobbed and weaved around obstructions in the road.

"Sure does," Keith said, flashing a portion of his teeth in a thin smile. "Why? It's not like he's gonna get a ticket for driving recklessly."

To punctuate his sentence, the driver hit another ghoul head-on. The desiccated body ripped in two, with the bottom half falling under the truck. It bounced around for a few seconds and then rolled out the rear tailgate, looking like it had been through a meat grinder.

The front half stuck to the front grille for another mile until, it too, fell under the truck to be pulped under the rolling tires.

Blood splatter covered the fender guards of the truck, the etched picture of a woman in a bikini all but covered in blood spray now.

The vehicle turned off the highway and started up a side road, the engine resonating off the abandoned houses on both sides of the street. Some had seen fire damage and were nothing more than blackened husks. Others seemed unharmed, as if the owner had locked the doors and had left for work and would return promptly at five-thirty.

The vehicle drove into the town square which was really a circle. A large circular expanse of grass and flowers filled the middle of the square and the road curved around it. The surrounding storefronts were filled with everything from a hair salon, to an insurance agency, to a comic book store. A video store across the square had faded posters hanging in its windows of the last movies to be released before the world fell apart. A sign in the middle of the dead grass of the rotary proclaimed: Welcome to Cliftondale Square, Saugus.

Pulling into the town square, the driver revved the engine even more. Henry looked at Keith and wondered if they were all mad.

"What the hell is he doing, he'll alert every dead bastard in the area!" Henry yelled at Keith.

"Yeah, I know, relax. Once the rotters come out, he's gonna drive off slowly. The rotters will follow him and we'll get a chance to see what's around here. So come on, we've got to hide before those smelly bastards see us."

Keith hopped off the back of the truck and Mark followed him, looking like the boy was ready to vomit from nerves. Henry and Jimmy followed soon after and hid in the bushes of what looked like a copy and fax store.

"You know, it's not a bad plan," Jimmy said, askance of Henry.

Henry frowned, but had to admit his friend was right. As long as the deaders were distracted, they'd be able to ransack the nearby stores with impunity.

The Ford revved its engine again and then hit the horn. The guard on the passenger side leaned out of the vehicle and yelled into the surrounding buildings.

"Come on, you fuckin' rotters, come to Daddy! Come on, you dead fucks, get your smelly asses out here!"

Henry heard a moaning sound, amplified by more vocal cords than he would have wanted to count. Then they started to appear. Most of the undead were months old if not some of the original ghouls from when the contaminated rains had first come. Stomachs were bloated and skin was dried like leather. One was missing its jaw, the orphaned tongue hanging low over its clavicle.

Another had a giant hole through its middle. Henry assumed from a gut shot at some time in the past. There were a few zombie soldiers mixed in with the group of walking corpses, their green uniforms now stained brown from dried blood. But it was the one woman ghoul that made Henry sit up and take notice and really be reminded of the Hell that was the world. The dead woman's age was unknown due to the deterioration of her body, but it was the dried husk of a baby she carried in her arms, the umbilical cord still attached to the baby's belly. The other end disappeared under the woman's skirt. The cord swayed back and forth with the shambling of the walking cadaver and

Henry felt a burning need to put a bullet in this one ghoul's head. But it was when he saw the baby twitch in the thin, skeletal-like arms, and the head turned his way, that he reached for his weapon, ready to end its miserable existence.

It was Jimmy who brought him to his senses.

Placing a hand on his arm with fingers of steel, Jimmy squeezed and hissed into his ear.

"What the fuck are you doing, Henry? If you shoot, they'll be on us in seconds. There's too damn many to take out before they'd be on us. Just be cool, they'll be gone soon."

Henry closed his eyes and tried to tune out the moaning and the whispering sound of the bodies moving around the town square.

The Ford started to drive out of the area, leading the ragtag flesh-eaters behind it like a sick parody of the Pied-Piper.

Minutes passed and soon the last walking corpse in line faded from view, nothing but the stench of death to signify they had been there at all.

"All right, let's go. Why don't me and Henry take the convenience store and Jimmy and Mark take the liquor store. Once you get anything useful, bring it out and set it over there on that pedestal in the center of the square. Once we're done, I'll call the guys back," he held up the two-way radio, "and we can wait for them up there. Then we'll load up and get the fuck out of Dodge."

Jimmy stood up and brushed leaves from his pants. "All right, sounds good to me. Come on, kid, let's do some looting." Then he headed off across the street to the liquor store with the boy behind him.

Henry and Keith stood up as well and Henry waved for Keith to go first. "After you, if you think after last night I'm gonna let you walk behind me than your shit out of luck."

Keith sneered at that, but started walking towards the store.

Damn, he thought. This guy is too goddamn smart. He's not going to let me get the drop on him. He looked over his shoulder to look at Henry, but the man wasn't smiling.

Oh well, there were other ways to kill a cat. He'd just bide his time a little longer. He just hoped Barry understood and didn't want to take the failure out of his hide.

With a slumping of his shoulders, Keith moved across the side of the street, with Henry behind him. Better to deal with the job at hand and worry about the other things later.

Besides, a lot could happen before they were safe inside the walls of the shopping mall again.

Oh yes, a lot could happen, indeed. That perked the security chief up a little and as he walked into the convenience store. His smile was back, although from his vantage point Henry couldn't see the man's bearded face.

With a jingling of a bell over the front door, the two men disappeared into the store, and silence descended over the square once again.

CHAPTER SEVENTEEN

VINNIE TUCCIE CLOSED the door to Barry's office and started down the stairs leading back to the food court. Stepping into the wide open area, he continued on to his destination at the opposite end of the mall.

As he walked through the mall, people would clear out of his path. The other residents of the mall knew about Vinnie, even if it was only by rumors.

The residents had decided with so many rumors about one man, at least some of them had to be true.

Wherever Vinnie went, people had a habit of disappearing.

As the large man walked through the halls, he smiled. He liked to be feared and had worked hard to establish his reputation long before the rains had come.

Before the world had fallen apart, Vinnie had worked for a small-time crime family living out of Boston. To say he was in the Mafia would have sounded cliché, even to his own ears. No, what was once the Mafia was long gone, to be replaced by opportunistic Americans, of all colors and nationalities.

It was only coincidence that Vinnie was Italian and had worked for an Italian crime boss. But Vinnie was the first person to keep those thoughts to himself. If other people wanted to think he was a Mafioso, then so be it. He figured it could only help to establish himself as a feared opponent of others.

He had been on a job in the suburbs of Boston almost six months ago to the day, he recalled. A client had owed his boss almost two g's and it had been Vinnie's job to visit the man and remind him of his obligations. Vinnie had just planned to break a few of the guy's fingers. Nothing too hard on the guy. The first visit was usually the easiest for both Vinnie and his client.

Things had gone well that day. The client had cried like a little baby and swore a check would be in the mail by the end of the day.

Satisfied, Vinnie left and had decided to grab a bite to eat in one of the diners on the highway.

That was when the first rains had fallen, and as Vinnie had sat on his stool in the restaurant, the people outside in the rain had fallen to the ground and twitched a little; and then had remained still.

The other people in the diner had freaked. Some had run into the rain to help the ones on the ground and then, they too, had collapsed to the wet asphalt.

Vinnie was bright enough to know it was a good idea to stay in the safety of the diner, to hell with the people outside. But it was when the people outside on the ground began to stand back up that things went from weird to downright crazy.

A man with an umbrella had climbed out of his car and was making a dash for the doors of the diner, but before he was three feet from the car, one of the other people outside had pulled him to the ground and had attacked him. Not such a big deal so far, Vinnie thought. Hell, he'd done that to countless people over his career. But it was when the attacker sank his teeth into the man on the ground and ripped the guy's throat out that Vinnie knew there was some strange shit going down.

Soon, others that were on their feet attacked the man and before Vinnie knew it, the entire group was pulling the man's clothes off to get at the flesh beneath. Arms and legs were fought over as the group of undead gorged themselves on the man's body. Sharpened nails from a woman's manicure ripped the man's stomach open. Internal organs and intestines were pulled out and quickly consumed, the ground under them nothing but a washed out red puddle due to the rain.

Vinnie watched the visceral scene in horror, not believing what he was seeing with his own eyes.

An hour later the rain stopped.

There was a tree in the lot and Vinnie could see a few birds lying dead on the ground under its wide branches. Off to the side of the diner, a dog was tied to a leash. It too, was either dead or sleeping and after all that rain, he doubted the animal could be sleeping. The radio in the diner started spouting emergency warnings about how something was causing a mass outbreak of violence. Police were even now attempting to round up the apparent crazy people and bring them to a place of safety for themselves and others that at the moment weren't infected.

What Vinnie didn't know was after the first rainstorm, police and fire services went out in droves to help anyone who needed it and to capture the raving maniacs.

Then the rain had started again. The men and women from the police and fire services were infected and then, they too, went on a murderous rampage. With the city helpless, the infrastructure soon collapsed and anarchy reigned.

What Vinnie also didn't realize at the moment while he was in the diner was that the outbreak had happened all across the United States and the world he knew was about to disappear forever.

He had stayed in the diner for the rest of the day and night along with the twelve others trapped inside. The ghouls had banged on the doors of the diner, wanting to feast on the living trapped inside, but the doors had held.

By daybreak of the next day, the rain had stopped and the sun was out again.

Unfortunately, so were the zombies. One of them had picked up a rock and had started to beat the glass door with it. The owner of the diner had said not to worry, that the door was made of hardened glass an inch thick, but Vinnie knew with enough determination the glass would break.

Two hours later that was exactly what happened. The ghoul had continued banging nonstop, its fingers nothing but bloody stumps from where the rock had pulverized the digits whenever the fingers had slipped in-between the glass and the rock. The zombie hadn't been smart enough to keep its fingers out of the way as the rock struck the glass and now the glass was covered in red smudges that slowly dripped down to the ground.

Vinnie watched as the first crack appeared in the glass, then another. Like a spider web growing from the middle, the cracks widened, until with one more hit, the glass shattered.

The safety glass fell to the ground with a tinkling sound, but it was drowned out by the moans of the undead and the screams of the diner's patrons.

Vinnie moved to the back of the diner and pulled his gun. It was a .45 pistol with a silver grip and he had used it for years. There were many murders still unsolved thanks to the weapon now in his hand. The pistol was completely untraceable. He watched as the patrons were attacked, the ghouls ripping into them like they were nothing more than cattle for the slaughter.

Most of the ghouls were occupied with feeding and Vinnie had decided now would be a good time to leave.

Darting for the back of the diner, he unlocked the small back door used for trash disposal and jumped out into the morning sun. He was blinded by the brightness and almost didn't see the zombie coming up on his right. Just before the dead man jumped him, Vinnie sidestepped away and shot the walking corpse in the chest. The man shook with the impact and he stopped his forward momentum, but within a heartbeat was back on the attack again. Vinnie squeezed the trigger twice, sending two more rounds into the man's upper body, one striking the heart and shredding the inside of his chest. The man shook with the impact of the rounds, but still continued forward.

Cursing under his breath, Vinnie raised the weapon and shot the guy through the head. This time the man pitched forward into the mud and remained still. Breathing a sigh of relief, he dashed to the front of the diner.

His Cadillac was out there and it was his only escape.

Rounding the diner, he saw the parking lot was clear, all the ghouls inside the diner feasting on the patrons. He darted for his car, and with a tense filled minute, pulled his keys from his pocket and unlocked the door. The sound of the alarm disengaging alerted a few zombies to his presence. Moving as one, they charged out of the diner and across the parking lot, their faces and clothes covered in blood and viscera.

Vinnie started his car and the eight-cylinder engine roared to life. He pulled out and headed for the highway. Two of the ghouls were heading right for him and he lined up the grille of the Caddy with the oncoming bodies.

Both bodies hit the Caddy dead center.

With the pulping of bones and flesh, they were knocked over like ten pins at the bowling alley.

Vinnie didn't stop.

Feeling the car drive over the bodies, he floored the gas pedal and surged over the corpses. One of the ghoul's heads became wedged in the tire well and another's arm lodge next to the muffler, the smell of burning meat and hair floating into the car, the odor making him gag. He turned the wheel and the head was dislodged. It rolled around in the tire well for a few more seconds and then shot off from the tire like a rocket, to land ten feet away. It rolled on the ground for a few seconds and came to a stop, the teeth gleaming in the sun. The man who had once owned those teeth had spent thousands to make them look as white and shiny as they did right now.

Vinnie swerved onto the highway and shot down the road like his car was on fire. But soon he calmed down a little and slowed to a more moderate speed. The highway was awash with carnage. Cars were on their sides and flames licked at what were once human beings. A tanker truck had rolled over onto its side when people had dashed across the highway trying to escape the chasing ghouls and now the entire road was blocked.

Now the tanker lay there quietly, the back slowly leaking its cargo of vegetable oil over the asphalt. The highway was blocked and the shoulder was covered in mud. Vinnie knew if he tried to get through there, his car would surely become trapped in the sludge. There were a few other cars around him, the people inside scared and having no idea what to do. He didn't care. He had learned from an early age to worry about himself and to hell with anyone else.

Backing up and turning around, he started driving up the highway in the wrong direction. Cars blared their horns at him and swerved out of the way, but Vinnie knew they too would mimic him soon enough, or abandon their vehicles to head out on foot.

Two miles down the highway, he took the on ramp and came out in a part of town he had never been to. The chaos could be seen here, also. Numerous houses were ablaze and there were bodies lying on the front lawns of some of the homes. The road led to a fork, the right side directing him to the Crystal Mall. He had taken it and had wound up in front of the large complex built to feed man's need for consumerism.

Leaving his car and walking to the double glass doors, he had tried to open them, but they were locked. Pounding on them, he was surprised and relieved when a Spanish man in his mid-forties walked down the long empty hallway. After using a large ring of keys to unlock the doors, the man had let him inside.

That had been his first meeting with Barry and he had become the man's partner ever since. Later, more people had arrived and soon a small community began to grow. When the first ghouls had arrived it had been decided that the mall needed to be fortified.

That was when Keith had risen to the front of the group and had helped to organize the chain-link fences over the doors. Vinnie had stepped back and let the bearded man take over. Vinnie preferred to be behind the scenes than out in front.

Now, months later, Vinnie was still doing what he did best, just for a different employer.

With Henry and Jimmy away on a foraging trip, Barry had instructed him to take care of Jeffrey and the two women. He was to do it silently and quietly. The rest of the enclave was ignorant of the true goings on in the mall.

And with the way Vinnie operated, it would stay that way.

CHAPTER EIGHTEEN

MARY WIPED THE sweat from her brow, the heat of the laundry room getting to her.

It was midmorning and her back was already aching from the manual labor.

The laundry was being done in the basement of the mall.

Large bathtubs had been setup, one next to the other, and water was carried in by buckets. There was a small fire lit with propane which was used to heat the water for the laundry and to boil away the deadly bacteria and other contaminates. Laundry soap was in abundance, raided from one of the stores in the mall.

Due to the amount of work it took to wash the clothes, all residents of the enclave had to wear their clothes until they were very dirty, bordering on filthy. The laundry smelled like death itself and Mary had to constantly control her from vomiting her breakfast.

Glancing over her shoulder at Cindy, she saw the young girl was fairing no better; the odor of sweat and unwashed bodies over-whelming.

The two had arrived a little after Henry and Jimmy had left on their foraging run. She would have preferred to have left with the men, but it appeared the mall had fallen into the 18th century and women were only good for laundry and cleaning. She was told that a special group of people did all the cooking.

So here she was, dropping another load of filthy clothing into the already dirty water.

The head woman in charge walked up behind Mary and placed her hand on Mary's shoulder.

"Cheer up, Mary, only two more hours until we break for lunch," Emma said.

Emma was a robust woman in her early fifties with bright red cheeks and red hair to match that looked like it had a mind of its own, the unruly mane constantly falling from the bun the woman would tie it into.

Mary's heart sank.

It already felt like she had been washing laundry for days.

Mary smiled at the older woman. "Great, can't wait."

Emma patted her shoulder again and moved on to see to another chore.

Cindy finished wringing out her last item in her latest batch of laundry and leaned closer to Mary.

"If Jimmy thinks I'm gonna do this for the rest of the winter, then he's crazy."

Mary nodded. "Tell me about it. Tell you what, when we see the boys tonight, we'll tell them what we think."

"What if they don't agree with us?" Cindy asked.

"Cindy, we're women. We'll make them see our way."

Cindy chuckled at that and the two continued working.

Two hours later, Mary left for a bathroom break. She had to walk down a long dank hallway in the basement until she came to a metal door. Inside was a toilet and a bucket of water next to it. Similar to Jimmy's experience, she used the facilities and then poured the bucket into the tank of the toilet. Then she flushed as normal.

When she was finished, she looked at herself in the mirror. Her hair was soaked with sweat and grime, and dirt covered her face and neck.

At the moment, she wouldn't be winning any beauty pageants, that was for sure, she thought.

Leaving the bathroom, she started walking back to the laundry area when a blur appeared in front of her eyes and she felt something wrap itself around her neck.

Like Henry had taught her, she tried to throw herself backward and elbow her attacker, but a knee pressed into the small of her back, keeping her body forward, while her neck was pulled back. The garrote squeezed even tighter around her neck and her vision began to fade. She struggled helplessly, the noose around her neck, and the knee in her back, continuing to keep her immobile. The pain was excruciating and tiny black spots appeared in front of her eyes as her brain screamed for oxygen. The blood pounded in her head and her knees gave out on her. She tried desperately to reach the .38 in her pants, but her attacker knocked her hand away and pulled the gun himself, tossing it away down the hall. Then her body stopped listening to her and she fell into a black void.

Falling into unconsciousness, she slumped to the floor.

Vinnie stepped away from the woman in front of him, breathing heavily. Behind him two guards were creeping up the hall.

He turned to them and pointed to Mary. "Damn, she can fight. She put up more of a struggle than most of the men I've taken down."

The two guards looked at Mary and then back to Vinnie.

"You know where to bring her, the same as the others when we get them, but be discreet. Barry doesn't want anyone to know where she's gone, especially her two armed friends." He bent over and picked up Mary's .38 from the hallway floor. Not a bad weapon, he thought, as he tucked it into his waistband. Then he followed the two guards down the hallway, Mary being carried between them.

He still had to get the blonde girl and the little man.

Pushing out his chest, he was sure they wouldn't be a problem.

*   *   *

Mary woke to whimpering.

She tried to stand up, but found she was tied to a chair. She looked to her left and saw Cindy sitting next to her. She, too, was tied to a chair. Mary could see the thin line around Cindy's neck where the garrote had cinched tight. More whimpering to her right. She turned to see Jeffrey spread out on a table. He was naked, his skin covered in goose bumps from the cold.

She looked around some more and realized they were in a room-sized refrigerator. The air was cold around her skin and she started to get goose bumps. She tried to talk, but realized she was wearing a gag, as was Jeffrey and Cindy.

She remembered Henry's tale about Keith showing up in the middle of the night and Henry's warning to watch their backs. She had thought she was doing a pretty good job of it, too.

Until right now, that is.

The large refrigerator door opened and Barry stepped in.

Behind him was a tall man, six-two at least. He had a long face and a nose that looked like it had been broken at least once in his life. The man wore a sneer that showed no mercy, his eyes a piercing blue and his black hair was slicked back like they used to do in the sixties.

Barry was smiling from ear to ear. "Hello, Mrs. Roberts. It's nice to see that you're awake finally. I'm so sorry for the unpleasantries. If I had a choice, you and your friends would have been gunned down out on the road long before all of this. But alas, my security chief is a coward and he decided to bring you back to us. All it took was to separate your little group and then grab you one by one.

In fact, even as we speak, your two male companions should be getting a bullet in the head. As for the three of you, well, I have much better uses for you. In fact, you're more valuable to me dead than alive."

Mary's eyebrows went up as she tried to puzzle over what the man was talking about. Cindy sent muffled curses at the man until the taller man walked over and slapped Cindy in the face. With tears running down her cheek, she went silent.

To her right, Jeffrey was straining to see what was going on.

Barry noticed this and nodded to the tall man.

"Vinnie, our friend on the table can't see. Would you place him in a better position to see what all the hubbub is about?" Barry asked, soothingly.

Vinnie went to Jeffrey and started to turn a wheel at the end of the table. Jeffrey's feet and the table slowly started to rise until Jeffrey was upside down on the table, his feet pointing up at the ceiling. The table was now vertical, the straps keeping Jeffrey from falling off. Almost immediately, the blood started to rush to Jeffrey's head and the man started to whimper behind his gag.

"You see, my dear Mrs. Roberts. May I call you Mary? We still have some small comforts here. I have acquired a few small generators to power my refrigerators and a few other necessities.

Mary sent daggers at him with her eyes, but Barry ignored her.

"You see, Mary, since everything fell apart, food has been hard to come by, and in fact a few months ago we were all near to starvation. Oh yes, we sent people out to forage, but do you have any idea how much food five-hundred-plus people consume in a single day, or a week? We, or should I say I, needed to come up with a way to feed us all before we all perished from starvation. At first I thought, why not eat the rotters. I mean, that's what they want to do to us, right? But the meat on their bodies is rotten and no one could figure out a way around that, so when we were low on food and desperate, we were blessed with a miracle. A small group of survivors were out on the highway. Keith had brought them back to us. On a whim, I shot one of them in the head and sent the body up to my personal cook. He sliced off the meat and made a wonderful stew. The bones were used to make soup, just as you would with any animal you killed for food. And I have recently decided to take it to the next level." He sneered malevolently.

"New world, new ways. In fact, you and your friends had some stew yesterday, I believe. I was very amused how Jeffrey over there seemed to really enjoy it."

Realizing what he had just said, Mary fought to keep her stomach settled. If she threw up now, she could very well drown in her own vomit.

"Although, almost all of the residents here have no idea what they're eating. They're just thankful they have it. And I'm happy to supply it. One must do what one must to survive."

Jeffrey started to squirm in his bonds, but they were too tight for him to get loose.

Barry's face grew serious and he nodded to Vinnie.

"Vinnie, would you please do the honors?"

"Yes, sir," Vinnie said.

First Vinnie pushed a large metal bucket under Jeffrey with his boot, and then he pulled a long hunting knife from the back of his pants.

Looking down at Jeffrey, the man grinned maliciously. "Sorry, pal, it's nothing personal." Then he brought the knife to Jeffrey's neck and drew it across the flesh, severing the carotid artery. Blood shot from the four inch long slice in Jeffrey's neck and sprayed Mary and Cindy. Both women went crazy, struggling with their bonds. Beside them, Jeffrey's eye's popped out of his head. As the seconds past, the blood stopped spurting and began to seep from the wound. The bucket collected the fluid until the drips became small drops that fell intermittently from the bottom of the table.

The tears ran down Mary's cheeks and she groaned behind her gag. Next to her, Cindy sobbed softly, shocked to see the butchery of their friend no more than three feet away.

Barry stood silently through the entire ordeal, not saying a word. Before the apocalypse, he had been a small man who ran a shopping mall. But now he held people's lives in his hand to do with what he wanted. To say Barry was drunk on power would be an understatement.

He walked over to Mary and leaned down so his face was no more than an inch from hers. Careful not to step in any blood, he whispered into her ear.

"Don't worry, dear, your friend will feed the mall for at least a day and a half; maybe two. And tomorrow, I'll be back for you and your beautiful friend. Until then, please enjoy your accommodations."

Vinnie retrieved a wheeled cart from the corner of the room, and after lowering the table, dragged Jeffrey's lifeless body onto it. Then, after covering the body with a sheet, he wheeled it out of the room.

Barry followed, and upon exiting the door, he stopped. Mary couldn't see his hand as the man was partially out of the door, but she heard the click and saw the walk-in refrigerator plunge into almost total darkness when Barry turned off the light. There was still a dull gloom of light filtering in from outside, however.

"Until tomorrow, ladies," he said and closed the door, throwing the room into perpetual darkness.

Mary sat there sobbing, while Cindy did the same next to her. If Barry was telling the truth, then Henry and Jimmy were already dead and she and her friend were trapped.

She struggled with her bonds, but they were too tight, cutting into her skin every time she tried to get loose.

As the minutes passed, the tears slowed. She had to get a hold of herself. If Henry and Jimmy were dead, then she had no one to rely on but herself, and she'd be damned if she was going to end up in a stew pot like a slaughtered deer.

With rage brewing in her gut, she wracked her brain for a way out. There had to be one, she just had to find it.

CHAPTER NINETEEN

WITH HIS .38 in hand, Jimmy opened the door for the liquor store. His shotgun was still back at the mall, safely hidden in the ceiling of the companion's alcove. He was really regretting it right about now.

Although the .38 should be more than enough to take down any ghouls in his way, he still would have preferred the piece of mind of having the stopping power of the shotgun.

His eyes scanned the interior of the store, the gloomy atmosphere making the hair stand up on the back of his neck. A thick layer of dust covered everything, his footsteps echoing off the lonely aisles. Glass and potato chip bags littered the floor. Many of the bottles had been knocked off their prospective shelves and had shattered, spilling their contents all over the polished linoleum, to later dry to a brown and sometimes black stain.

From the looks of the store, at least a few people had done some looting.

But there was still more than enough for the two men.

Mark stood directly behind him, patiently waiting to be told what to do.

"So, what do you usually get from a liquor store? Besides the obvious," Jimmy asked the boy.

"Well, we get all the hard stuff, for one. Its good for cuts and stuff and the security men get a lot of stuff in trade for it."

Jimmy nodded. "Yeah, well if I'm risking my ass so some guard can make a buck, then there'll be hell to pay, I'll tell you that."

Mark just shrugged. "I don't know what to tell you, I just do what I'm told."

"Yeah, I know, kid, sorry. Tell you what, grab a carriage and start getting what you need, I'll watch your back."

"Okay," Mark said, and after grabbing a shopping cart, started to move around the aisles grabbing bottles off the shelves.

Jimmy jumped up onto the counter and watched the boy move from aisle to aisle. From his vantage point, he could see everything and was easily able to keep an eye on Mark. Sitting on the counter by Jimmy's feet was a small box of imitation Swiss Army knives. Jimmy had always wanted one as a kid, but his dad just had never gotten around to getting him one. With a slight smile to his lips of things in the past, he bent over and grabbed one.

Not wanting to take his eyes off Mark, he slipped it into his sock under the cuff of his pants. His dad had always carried the one he had owned in his boot and Jimmy now duplicated his father out of sheer habit. The knife felt cold against his skin, but then it slowly began to warm up. The three inch knife was forgotten as Jimmy stood up to watch Mark move through the aisles.

When Mark was finished, Jimmy hopped down to the floor.

"All right, if you're full, then let's bring this stuff outside and come back for another load," Jimmy said, moving to the door.

Mark grinned and headed for the exit.

"Hold it, kid, let me go first. Then if it's clear, I'll wave you out."

"Okay, sure, whatever you want," Mark said, moving aside so Jimmy could exit the building. Mark was a little more relaxed now, as things were going smoothly.

Stepping out into the sunlight, Jimmy checked the area. The four foot walkway that led up to the liquor store had three and a half foot high shrubs lining both sides, although now they were growing wild after months of being left unattended.

Satisfied the coast was clear, Jimmy waved the boy out.

Mark pushed the cart onto the walkway and started to the street, with Jimmy a few feet in front of him.

While Mark walked, he wasn't able to see the head that poked through the bushes no more than a foot off the ground. As he walked by the head, it jumped out farther and raised itself up. Coming from behind, it jammed its head between the boy's legs, its teeth sinking into his inner thigh. The first bite ripped his pants enough for the teeth to sink into the flesh beneath. Jaws ripped into his thigh and he tripped and fell to the ground with a startled yell of surprise and pain.

The ghoul had severed a major artery in the boy's leg, the blood gushing into the cadaver's mouth. Jimmy turned at the yell, startled at the attacking corpse climbing on the boy. What was most startling was the fact the ghoul had no lower half.

Everything below the waist was missing, and as the animated cadaver moved, parts of its insides drooped onto the ground.

Jimmy ran over to the boy, taking the scene in less than a second. With his left hand, he grabbed the rotting head by the hair, and with his right, he placed the .38's muzzle next to the ghoul's ear. Then he squeezed the trigger.

The bushes were covered in brains and bits of red as the ghoul dropped to the sidewalk, half its skull now missing. Jimmy pulled the bifurcated body out of the way, and after a quick look around to make sure the area was clear of other attackers, he leaned down to help Mark.

But the moment Jimmy saw the kid's wound, he knew it was too late. The blood was pumping from between the wound with every beat of Mark's heart. Even if Jimmy was able to get a tourniquet on the leg, there was no one with the skill to sew the artery back together, nor would there be a way to replace the missing blood that was now spread out on the concrete.

Those days were gone.

Mark was already weak from blood loss and his eyes were getting droopy.

Jimmy took off his jacket and placed it under the boy's head to try to make him more comfortable.

"I'm so sorry, kid. I was supposed to watch your back," Jimmy said, kneeling down next to Mark.

Mark smiled a little. "That's okay, it's not your fault. I wasn't made for this kind of stuff, but they made me go. I would have gotten it sooner or later anyway." He paused for a moment. "Look, I'm tired. I think I'll take a nap," he said softly.

With a tear in his eye, Jimmy smiled. "Sure, kid, that's okay. You rest and before you know it we'll be back at the mall, safe and sound."

Mark closed his eyes for the last time. Jimmy stayed next to the boy for another minute, feeling the loss of another life. He might not have known the boy long, but Jimmy was pretty sure they would have been friends. And on top of all that, a brief memory of Scott floated to the forefront of his mind, but he pushed it back down, not wanting to deal with it at the moment. His guilt had been hard to bear and it had taken months for him to accept he wasn't entirely at fault at the death of his friend back at Pineridge Labs.

Jimmy stood up and walked to the edge of the walkway. One lone ghoul was shambling into the square, but it was a ways off and not much of a threat yet. He guessed the decoy vehicle only worked for so long.

Every now and then he'd hear a rifle shot float over the other buildings, the two coldhearts in the Ford having some fun.

Then he heard the carriage roll behind him and he turned around to see Mark slowly standing up. His face was slack and his eyes were a milky white, the blue now gone.

He tried to talk, but nothing came out but a guttural sound.

Jimmy stood there in shock.

"What the fuck?" He gasped in shock, watching the boy shambling toward him with a limp, his treacle-like movements making him look like he was walking underwater.

"Mark, are you all right? Shit, buddy, I thought you were dead."

But Mark was beyond listening as he stumbled toward Jimmy. While this was a first for Jimmy, he quickly realized that the boy had come back after being killed by the crawling ghoul.

Jimmy took one step back and raised his .38. He knew what he had to do, but was still shocked at what had just transpired.

When you were killed by the walking dead, you stayed dead.

That's it, the end.

People didn't get back up like in a cheesy 1980s horror movie. That would be ridiculous.

But then again, the world being turned into animated corpses in the first place, by contaminated rain, no doubt, was pretty far fetched, also.

Mark was only two feet away from him and Jimmy snapped out of it. With a sigh, he lined up the boy's head and then put a hole in his forehead. Mark's head snapped back and the rear of his skull exploded onto the sidewalk, the boy's hair seeming to fly up and away from his scalp from the force of the bullet. His body fell to the concrete, this time dead for good.

Jimmy grabbed the carriage, and with one more glance at Mark, pushed it into the center where Keith had told him to go.

Shaking his head, he still tried to wrap his head around what had just happened. "Oh man, Henry is not going to believe this shit," he muttered to himself

CHAPTER TWENTY

THE CONVENIENCE STORE was in a similar state of disrepair as the liquor store. Crushed cans of food and old discarded candy wrappers littered the floor. Once more, the tops of the items were covered with a fine layer of dust.

The front door closed behind the two men and Henry surveyed the area around him. For the moment it was quiet, although that could change at any second. The stench of death filled the inside of the store, but whether it was from something animated or long dead was unknown.

Keith was already moving through the aisles, his rifle in front of him in his right hand. His left was tossing food into a basket he was kicking across the floor.

Keith shifted his attention to Henry and pointed over to the next aisle.

"Why don't you go over there. Grab all the canned goods. This is my second time here, and if I have my way, it'll be the last."

Henry nodded and reached down and picked up a basket. Moving to the next aisle, he began dropping canned goods into his basket. Once he had filled it, he went back to the front and retrieved another. He did this multiple times until there were more than ten baskets sitting by the door, waiting to be carried outside.

Off to the right was the counter where the clerk would have taken up residence. Henry noticed a small rack on the counter with cigarette lighters in it. Behind the rack, the spaces where the cigarette cartons would have sat were all empty.

Evidently, when people started to panic, it was their smokes they were the most scared of running out of. Henry needed a new lighter and he was sure Jimmy wouldn't say no to one, either. So he set down his full basket and moved toward the counter, while the sounds of Keith rattling around in the back of the store drifted across the aisles.

Reaching over the counter to retrieve a lighter, he was startled when a hand reached over and grabbed his arm from behind the counter. Then a pallid face appeared and rose up.

The head was a rotting mass of maggots. Only one eye still remained, the empty other socket nothing but a dark cavity. Brown teeth gleamed in the gloom of the store as the jaws darted for Henry's arm.

Henry ripped his arm away from the counter, the fingers breaking off the hand.

The rotting stench filled his nose and he realized this was what he must have first detected when he'd first entered the store.

The ghoul moved around the side of the counter and lunged for Henry. Calmly, Henry raised his Glock and sent a bullet through the mottled cranium. The head jerked from the impact and the body slumped to the floor. Henry stepped over the corpse and retrieved the lighters, then turned in time to see Keith moving up the aisle with his hands full of goods.

Henry shook his head at the mistake the man was making.

If Keith had needed to use his weapon, his hands would be hopelessly tied up with the supplies in his arms and he would never have a chance.

But the store was empty and Keith made it to the front easily. He looked down at the dead body with the massive hole in its head and smirked.

"Found one, huh? Yeah, they like to hide in the corners of the stores. They wait and then they jump out at ya," Keith said.

Henry frowned. "Well, thanks for passing on that nugget of knowledge."

Keith saluted him. "Happy to help, now what do you say we get this shit outside. The boys should be back with our transportation out of here at any minute."

Henry answered by picking up a basket-full of cans and opening the door and walking outside.

Jimmy was already waiting for them, and as Henry moved across the quiet street, he noticed Jimmy was alone. When Henry moved closer, he noticed Jimmy looked upset.

"Hey, buddy, what's up? Where's the kid, where's Mark?" Henry asked, setting his load down onto the ground next to the carriage full of booze.

Jimmy looked into Henry's eyes. "He's dead, a deader got him. Came out of the bushes and bit him in the thigh. The kid bled out. He never had a chance, but that's not the worst of it."

Henry waited for the rest and when Jimmy just stood there, he prodded him to continue.

"Yeah, and?"

"And, once the kid died and I started to leave, he got back up again and tried to attack me. Henry, he was a fuckin' deader."

"What? That's ridiculous. You don't come back if you're bit," Henry scoffed

Keith moved up behind Henry and set his two baskets down on the cement.

"What are you guys talking about, where's Mark?"

"Dead," Jimmy said. "Then he got back up again as one of them."

"Yeah, so what? That's what happens if you get bit by a rotter. Shit, it's been like that for more than two months now. Where the hell have you guys been?" Keith asked.

"Midwest mostly, then we started traveling north, why?" Henry asked.

"Well, about two months ago one of the guys on patrol got bit. He died from the infection. It wasn't long after he died that he got back up and attacked some other people. He killed two and wounded another. An old woman if I remember correctly. She died from her wounds, too, and sure enough, she came back. But that time we were ready and Barry personally put a bullet in her head."

"Shit, I was afraid of this. The damn virus or infection or bacteria that made the dead walk has mutated. Now it can be transferred from carrier to victim. The rain water doesn't matter anymore," Henry said.

Keith snorted. "The rain? Hell, that's been fine for almost a month now. You still have to boil it if you want to drink it, but if you get caught out in the rain, you don't end up dead. Maybe a little sick."

"No shit? The rain's not contaminated anymore?" Jimmy asked amazed.

"Well, I can't say everywhere, but it's been better around here. We had a scientist with us a few months ago and he said it had something to do with the atmosphere and the ozone layer and that the rays of the sun could destroy the bacteria. Something like that. He also said it might have to do with the temperature dropping, something about the bacteria only being able to survive in warmer climates. I'm not sure, really. I'm not too good at the scientific stuff."

The roar of an engine drifted across the town square and the three men looked up.

"Looks like our rides here," Keith said with a grin.

The ghoul Jimmy had seen earlier had finally stumbled a little closer to the three men than Henry would have preferred, so raising his Glock, he shot the shambling corpse in the head. The body fell back to the street as if a giant hand had pushed it over. The arms and legs twitched for a moment, as if the body didn't yet know the brain was destroyed, then the limbs lay still.

The Ford truck roared into the square, the two men inside whooping it up like a couple of cowboys. With a screeching of tires, the truck pulled up next to the three men and the driver jumped out.

"Hey, Keith, you ready? Those rotters chased us all over the place. But a few changed direction. I figure they'll be coming back here real soon. Any trouble?"

Keith shook his head. "Sorry, Rob, so far it's been quiet, well sort of."

Rob looked at the three men and then he looked around the square.

"Hey, where's Mark?" He asked.

"Dead, rotter got him," Keith stated.

Some of the joviality left Rob's face. "No shit? That sucks, man. I kind of liked the kid. Oh, well, when it's your time and all that, I guess, huh?" He asked looking to Henry.

Henry stared at the man, silently wanting to put a bullet through the blowhard's face.

"Yeah, sure, whatever. Look, let's get this stuff loaded and get the hell out of here," Henry said. Looking around the square, more of the undead were arriving, attracted to the gunfire, talking and the rumble of the truck's engine.

Rob smiled. "Sure, no prob." Then he retrieved a basket and started loading the goods into the rear bed of the truck.

Keith grinned when he saw the carriage of liquor. Picking up a bottle of Vodka, his smile grew from ear to ear.

"Nice, I'm gonna give this one to Barry, he likes Vodka," Keith said, handing the bottle to the other man in the truck.

"That's great, just make sure to tell him a man died so he could drink his Vodka." Jimmy said with a harshness in his voice Keith immediately picked up on.

Keith turned to look at Jimmy, the passenger in the truck already bringing his weapon down against the frame of the window.

Henry jumped in. "He doesn't mean anything. He just meant that a good kid gave his life for all that booze, that's all. Right, Jimmy?"

Jimmy looked into Henry's eyes and saw that Henry didn't want the argument to continue. Then Henry mouthed the word "Please," so that only Jimmy could see.

Jimmy switched his attention away from Henry back to Keith, his voice now at a more civil tone.

"Yeah, that's what I meant. Didn't mean anything by it. Sorry."

Keith relaxed a little. "Sure, man, it's cool."

Moaning drifted to the group of men and they turned as one to see a large group of undead entering the town square.

Rob threw the last basket of food into the truck, ran around to the driver's seat and hopped in.

"Here they come. They weren't too far away from us. They moved quicker than I thought," Rob said, revving the engine.

"That's cool, Rob. We're done for today. You two, help me toss the booze into the back and then let's go," Keith asked Henry and Jimmy.

Both men answered by grabbing bottles and setting them in the truck. One minute later, with the first of the ghouls only a few feet away, the men climbed into the truck's tailgate. Keith slapped the roof of the cab twice and yelled to Rob.

"Let's go, we're done."

With the surging of the vehicle, Rob took off. The front grille of the Ford plowed into the crowd of plodding bodies, sending them flying in all directions. Canned goods and liquor bottles rolled around Henry's feet when the truck took a turn to wide. After a second, the driver regained control and took off down the road, leaving the town square full of the undead behind; only the wails of the zombie's moans following the truck as it sped away.

The truck cruised up the road, the sun high overhead. Henry and Jimmy sat in the back of the truck with the wind biting into them. Jimmy had it worse as he had left his jacket with Mark. Once they returned to the mall, though, it would be a simple matter to requisition another one, but until then, he had to grit his teeth and bare the cold.

Time went by and soon the mall came into view. The truck took the off-ramp and soon the pinger was activated and the truck waited patiently for the undead crowd to move away from the loading dock's bay doors.

A few wandered too close and were quickly dispatched by the men in the truck.

When the all-clear was given, the Ford slowly drove into the loading dock. Once through, the doors slammed shut and the pinger was switched off.

Within ten minutes of the pinger being turned off, the mall was surrounded by a wave of walking dead once again.

The shopping mall became an island of the living surrounded by a sea of the undead.

CHAPTER TWENTY-ONE

HENRY JUMPED DOWN off the rear of the truck, with Jimmy following close behind. No sooner had the truck pulled in then a group of people started to unload the supplies.

Henry and Jimmy stopped and waited at the top of the ramp for Keith. The bearded man walked over to the two friends and pointed to a door that opened out to the long hallway leading back to the living spaces in the mall.

"You guys can leave, we're done for today. Tomorrow we'll roll out again, but to a different town. Lately, we've had to go farther out to get supplies, though."

"What about all the stuff we left behind at the town square?" Jimmy asked. "Aren't you gonna go get it?"

Keith nodded. "Hell, yeah, when we're done, that place will be stripped bare. Another group will go out a little later. They'll clean up what we missed. If there's one thing we've learned how to do around here, it's using everything we can to survive. See you guys later. I need to go report in to Barry."

Henry watched the man leave. "Yeah, see ya," he said.

Henry waited for the door to close behind Keith and then he turned to Jimmy.

"You know what? I can't get a read on that guy. One second I think he wants to kill me and the next he acts like he's our friend," Henry said, looking confused.

"Couldn't tell ya, I only know what you've told me," Jimmy said, starting for the door. "I'm hungry, I'm gonna get something to eat."

"Okay, I'll see you later. I'm feeling a little restless. I think I'll walk around a little bit, check this place out some more."

Jimmy paused at the door. "So, what do you think? Do we have problems coming our way?"

Henry frowned. "Probably, but for now just keep your head up and watch your back. This may not be such a great place after all. We'll just have to wait and see. If anything's to it then let them make the first move, we'll be ready."

"But I thought they already did, last night," Jimmy stated.

"Yeah, but as I was there to stop whatever they had planned, I don't count it. Just stay on your guard," Henry told him

Jimmy nodded and with a wave went through the door leading to the mall.

Henry stood in the loading dock for another minute, watching the men and women offloading the food and liquor. One of the women saw him looking and flashed him a smile. He reciprocated with one of his own and then left the loading dock with an unsettling feeling in his stomach.

Henry watched the people inside the mall as he walked through the hallways. There were all colors and nationalities represented. Old and young alike had taken refuge inside the stone walls.

Sometimes when he passed some of the residents, he would get a smile or a nod. But usually he was ignored. Turning a corner, he saw a large group of children. They were all leaving a store that had once sold cheese and spices. Now it was used as the school. Henry slowed as he approached. Mothers and a few fathers were blocking the hall as they milled about waiting to pick up their children from school.

Little boys and girls ran out and into the arms of loving parents or sometimes older siblings. Henry watched all this in a sort of a daze. It was all so surreal. While the world died outside the walls of the mall, inside life was moving forward.

When the last child had left, skipping down the hallway, holding his mother's hand in his, Henry walked up to the makeshift school.

Inside was Mrs. Willis.

Upon seeing her again, Henry felt a fluttering in his stomach he hadn't felt in over twenty years. Being older and wiser, he had the confidence to step inside the room and clear his throat, overcoming the nervousness he felt.

Mrs. Willis turned around to see him standing there. "May I help you?" She asked from in front of the chalkboard that had been salvaged from the toy store in the mall.

Henry's confidence dried up the second she looked at him. He felt like a high school boy again as he went up to the girl he liked, wanting to ask her to the prom.

"Ah, hi. I'm Henry. I'm new here. Me and my friends just arrived yesterday," he said, nervously.

She smiled at him, the smile carrying up to her blue-green eyes. "Don't you mean; my friends and I just arrived yesterday?"

For a moment Henry didn't understand what she was saying and then it clicked. Embarrassed, he looked down at the floor. "Oh, yes, of course, sorry."

"Not at all, I'm just teasing. After teaching children all day it becomes kind of a habit. Please, sit down," she said, motioning for him to take a seat. The room was filled with kitchen chairs taken from a furniture store in the mall. The chairs were all lined up in neat little rows. Henry picked one on the end, near Mrs. Willis's desk.

She held out her hand. "I'm Gwen," she said with a flash of white teeth.

Henry shook her hand gently. "And I'm Henry, oh wait, I already said that didn't I. Look, I'm a little nervous, I'm not used to talking to women. I was married for more than twenty years."

"Oh, may I ask where your wife is now?"

Henry's voice grew distant as he remembered the past. "She's dead, got infected. I had to kill her myself."

Gwen moved from behind her desk and sat down next to him. "I'm so sorry, if its any consolation, I too, lost my husband a few months ago."

Henry looked up. "Did he become infected, too?"

She shook her head. "No, would you believe he cut himself with a rusty knife. He had just killed one of those creatures and he accidentally cut himself. Later, it got infected. There weren't any antibiotics to be found. A few days after that he developed a fever and the wound turned gangrenous. Then he died." She smiled wanly.

"Funny, before all this happened he would have received a shot of Penicillin and it would have cleared right up, instead he died. It's like we now live in the middle-ages again."

Henry nodded. "I know what you mean. Things we used to take for granted are gone forever."

The two sat there in the schoolroom for a while, the silence comfortable. The two had bonded over a similar loss, and as the hours rolled by, Henry became closer to Gwen. They had similar interests and were close to the same age. They talked for hours about how life was and what they hoped it would be. Before Henry knew it, it was late and he realized he was starving.

"Wow, look how late it is. I should get back to my friends," he said, checking his watch.

She nodded. "Yes, I still need to grade some tests the children took and there are some other matters I need to attend to."

"Oh, like what?" Henry asked curious.

She frowned, not sure if she should tell him, but then her eyes perked up, her decision made. "Some of the parents have told me about people who have gone missing. One day they're here and the next, gone. All their belongings and clothes vanish with them, too. Some of the parents have gone to the security men, but they just shrug it off and say that some people decide to move on and leave here. But if that's true, then where would they go? I did some checking and it's been going on for months. Our population is slowly shrinking and Barry doesn't seem to care. The worst thing is, none of us knows what to do about it. Could you help me? Please?"

Henry placed his hand on hers. "Of course I'll help. Let me do some digging and I'll let you know what I find out. Some of the guards have big mouths; I should be able to get something out of one of them."

"Oh thank you, Henry", she said, leaning over and giving him a hug. Then realizing what she'd done, she quickly pulled away.

"Oh, I'm sorry, it's just…"

Henry smiled at her. "No, it's okay, actually. I liked it."

She smiled bashfully. "So did I."

Henry took the initiative and looked into her eyes. "Look, after dinner, can we get together again and, you know, talk some more?"

Her eyes sparkled. "I'd like that."

Henry stood up, still holding her hand. He let it go and stepped away, moving toward the exit. "I'll see you later then?"

She nodded. "Count on it."

Henry turned and walked out of the room. He decided he'd head back to his berth and change into some fresh clothes. One advantage to living in a mall was the abundance of clothing. Walking down the hallways, he felt like he was sixteen again and in love. The two of them had made a connection, whether it was because of mutual loss or just a physical thing, he felt himself already looking forward to seeing Gwen again.

With a skip to his step and a whistle on his lips, he headed off to change.

It looked like things were looking up.

Chapter Twenty-two

Jimmy walked down a side hallway on his way to the food court. He was starving, the exertions of the day kicking his digestive system into overdrive. He had snagged a candy bar from the supplies on the way back to the mall, but it was doing little to curb his growing appetite.

Hearing a muffled cry, he slowed as he walked by a side hallway. The hall was only four feet wide and seemed to go on forever, the end lost in the shadows of the building.

The cry sounded again, softer this time. Drawing his .38, he called out.

"Hello, anyone there? Are you okay?"

There was nothing, no reply.

If someone was in trouble either they couldn't answer or wouldn't. Checking his surroundings, he noticed he seemed to be in a remote part of the shopping mall. The stores surrounding him were unoccupied, the contents long removed and divided amongst the people of the enclave.

Slowly, he moved into the small tunnel. Pipes overhead and exposed wires signified the long hallway must be some kind of service access. The deeper he went, the darker it became, the illumination barely penetrating the gloom.

He spotted a shadow in front of him, no more than six feet away.

With his weapon in hand he crept closer.

"Hey, what's the matter? Do you need help?"

Then the figure stood up and pulled off the cloak covering its head. Standing in front of him was one of the security guards. Jimmy recognized him from earlier in the day when he had walked through the mall. Before Jimmy could ask what was going on, he felt something heavy hit the back of his head just above his neck. Darkness flooded his vision and he fell to the floor, unconscious.

Another man came out of a small recess in the side of the hallway. A small patch of light framed his face for just a moment.

Vinnie smiled as he looked down at the prone figure of Jimmy. He looked over at the guard, his smile turning to a sneer.

"You see how it's done? Stealth and guile, that is how you take out an enemy. Now pick him up and bring him to join his two female friends. Once I take the other one down, they can all have a reunion before they die."

Nodding, the guard picked Jimmy up with a grunt and dragged him deeper into the tunnel. There was a laundry cart at the end where the guard could place Jimmy and then wheel him through the mall, with none the wiser.

Vinnie was already gone, on his way to set a trap for Henry. He wasn't worried; Vinnie had killed more men than he could count.

What kind of a threat could a middle-aged man hold for him?

The answer was none.

Turning the corner, Vinnie stepped out into the lighted mall, the skylights letting in the bright sunshine. Residents stepped out of his way, knowing his reputation as Barry's enforcer. He smiled at that. These people had no idea of his true duties, but let them think what they wanted. After all, it kept them in line.

And that was how he liked it.

Henry arrived at his berth hours after Jimmy had been attacked and captured. Unaware of his friend's predicament, he stepped into his alcove, prepared to change his clothing.

He was about to reach for a candle to give himself some much needed light when his instincts sensed someone else was in the room with him. The vague scent of the person and stifled breathing came to him.

There was someone behind him!

Henry whirled when a shadow passed over his face and he raised his right hand in front of his face. He felt something burn against his wrist and then his arm was pinned against his neck as the garrote tightened around his neck.

Henry threw himself backward against his attacker, ramming him against the glass doors. The glass shook in its frame, but held.

He swung his free arm outward and bent at the waist, sending his assailant flying over his hip. The man was huge and yet he fell into the toss, not resisting Henry in any way. Henry leaned over and felt the garrote scrape his nose and face as he slipped out of the noose. But the noose cinched tighter around his arm and Henry realized the man had let himself be thrown. Now, the man pulled, using his own body weight, dragging Henry by the noose cinched tight around his wrist.

Henry hit the ground hard, but managed to roll to soften the blow. Then the man was on top of him. Henry punched the shadowy attacker in the chest to try and give himself some breathing room. Then he reached down and tried to pull his Glock. His attacker seized his wrist and wrenched the weapon out of his hand. The Glock went spinning away across the floor, out of reach for now. The noose around his wrist loosened for a moment as his attacker reached down and grabbed his shirt, both hands in the material. Before Henry realized it, he was sent sailing over the man's shoulder. He hit the floor and his back came up against the wall. For a moment, Henry saw sparks in his eyes, then shaking his head to clear it; he reached down and pulled the large panga riding his hip.

The blade slid free of its sheath, his opponent pausing at the sound.

The two men stood across from each other in the gloom of the alcove, their breathing coming in gasps from their exertion. The light silhouetted Henry's opponent. He was a large man, at least six feet, and in the gloom Henry could see the man's hair was slicked back, although at the moment half was a ruffled mess.

Worried thoughts floated through Henry's head. If this man was attacking him, then what of his friends? Were they safe or had they already been captured? And if so, why, what did Barry have to gain in this maneuver?

The dull metal of the Glock gleamed across the room. Henry still had the .38 in the small of his back, the weapon miraculously still there, but he knew if he reached for it, the moment it would take to draw it, his attacker would be on him. He'd already witnessed the man's speed.

Suddenly, the man lunged at him. Henry swiped at the man's arm with the panga, the knife slicing into his attacker's forearm.

But it had been a ruse!

The man let himself be cut as he stepped closer to Henry. The man's fingers sank into Henry's arm. Henry felt the nerves in his hand go numb and watched as his hand opened and the panga slid to the floor with a dull clang.

Before his attacker could move, Henry drove his knee up and into the man's stomach with everything he had. He heard the large man grunt, but he reached out, grabbing Henry's other arm. Henry tried to knee him in the groin, but the man blocked it skillfully. Henry tried to pull away, but his attacker only tried to yank him back.

Suddenly, Henry let himself be pulled forward, and then he bent back his head and slammed his forehead down onto the man's nose. He heard the satisfactory sound of cartilage breaking. Henry's vision exploded with light, the trauma to his head only less intense than what he'd just done to his attacker.

He felt the man's grip weaken on his arm and he pulled away. The attacker stumbled away, raising his hand to his shattered nose. With an opponent as powerful as the one in front of him, Henry knew he could show no mercy, nor did the man deserve any.

Sending a roundhouse punch into the man's jaw, his opponent stepped back another foot. That gave Henry the valuable second he needed to retrieve his panga. Reaching down and retrieving it, he swung his leg around and struck his attacker in the stomach with his boot heel. The man doubled over, but quickly regained his composure.

But it was too late.

Henry stepped to the man's side and then brought the panga down in an overhead chop. The blade sliced into muscle and spine, severing nerve endings. Before the man hit the floor, he was paralyzed. Blood pooled onto the floor and Henry stepped aside and rolled the man over.

"Where are my friends? What have you done with them? Are they okay? Talk, damn you!"

Vinnie was lying supine on the floor. His mouth tried to move, but the nerves were severed. He breathed a few more times and then his chest stopped moving. Blood dripped from the corner of his mouth to mingle with what was already on the floor.

Cursing, Henry stood up and kicked the man in the ribs. He looked up to the sound of footsteps running his way.

"Shit," he muttered to himself.

Grabbing his Glock and sheathing his panga after a quick wipe to clean it on Vinnie's shirt, he looked around for a place to run. He was tired and had just had the shit knocked out of him. He needed to hide and weigh his options.

Looking up at the ceiling, he remembered the shotgun and other weapons secluded up there. Pulling a chair to him, he pushed open the ceiling panel. Sure enough, there was a crawl space, and off in the gloom there was a vent for heating and air conditioning. He quickly grabbed one of the packs on the floor in the corner. Pulling his body into the ceiling, he kicked the chair away.

Replacing the tile, he crawled into the vent, and with shotgun in tow, shimmied into the two-foot wide duct.

As he turned a corner and started down an open expanse of ductwork, he could hear the guards cursing and tearing the place apart looking for him. Startled cries floated up into the vent, once Vinnie was found.

Then the voices were lost as Henry scurried deeper into the ventilation system.

If his friends were still alive, he would find them. And their captors would be showed no mercy.

That, he would bet his life on.

CHAPTER TWENTY-THREE

KEITH CAME CHARGING into Henry's room. But instead of seeing the man lying on the ground dead, he saw Vinnie with the back of his neck cut.

The enforcer's face showed the bruises he had received from Henry. Keith looked all around the room with the help of two other guards, but the outsider was nowhere to be found.

"Shit, he has to be here. You two," he said pointing to the two other guards, "go in the back and make sure he's not hiding back there. If you see him, shoot on sight. Enough of this sneaking around bullshit. I want that man dead! Now move!"

The others nodded and ran to the back of the store. There was a storage room back there where the merchant who had originally occupied the store had kept extra merchandise. It was possible Henry was hiding in there.

Three minutes later the guards returned.

"There's no sign of him, we looked everywhere, I swear," the first guard said.

"Besides," the second guard said, "there aren't that many places to hide back there. If he was back there we would have found him."

Keith stood fuming for a few minutes while the two guards waited, fidgeting the whole time. His eyes seethed with anger, his body trembling with rage.

"Dammit, all right fine. You, go tell the others in security. I want that man found," he said to the first guard. "Shoot on sight. If any of the residents ask, tell them that Henry killed a mother and child or something like that. And you," he said, pointing to the other guard. "You go get a container for Vinnie here. Bring him to the kitchens, might as well get some use from his death."

The two guards still stood there.

Keith stared at them as if they were idiots. "Well, what the hell are you waiting for? Get going."

"Oh, sorry, we didn't know you were done. Yes, sir, we're gone," the first guard said. Then they both took off into the hallway on their individual tasks.

Keith stared at Vinnie's body for another minute. He had to admit that Henry had done him a favor by taking out the large Italian. Frankly, Keith had never had the balls to mess with the man. But that still didn't change anything. Henry was a loose end that needed to be cut. The shopping mall wasn't that big, sooner or later one of his guards would see him, and then the man would be his.

Keith exited the store and strolled away down the hall.

He had an appointment with Barry and at least they had the other outsiders, so Barry shouldn't be too upset.

A smirk crossed his lips when he thought of what was to come.

Oh, yes, he was going to enjoy what was coming next.

*　　*　　*

Jimmy awoke to water in his face.

Blowing the cold liquid from his nose and mouth, he opened his eyes to see Barry and Keith standing over him. Sitting next to him was Mary and Cindy, both still gagged and tied. Both seemed scared, although appeared to be unharmed; their eyes were red and wet from crying

"What the fuck is going on here!" Jimmy growled at Barry.

"I'd watch my tongue if I were you, boy. I'll be asking the questions here," Barry stated.

"Fuck you, you fuckin' spic. I'm not telling you shit!" Jimmy yelled.

"Now, now, there's no need for name calling. Do it again and I'll cut out your tongue. Try me if you don't believe me."

Jimmy saw Barry's eyes and realized the man wasn't bluffing.

Jimmy's shoulders sagged a little and he looked up at Barry.

"Fine. What do you want? Why the hell are we tied up like this?" Jimmy spit.

"That's better. Don't you know you can get more flies with honey than with vinegar?"

Jimmy grimaced. "Jesus Christ, you really are crazy. Both you and your sidekick over there," Jimmy said, using his chin to point to Keith.

Keith stepped over to Jimmy and slapped the younger man hard against the face. Jimmy rolled with the hit, but he still felt his brain rattle in his head.

Jimmy grinned at the man. "Tough guy, let's see how tough you are if I get out of this chair!" Jimmy yelled. Keith was starting to raise his hand to Jimmy again, but Barry held him back.

Then Barry stepped forward to stand in front of Jimmy.

"I want to know where your friend Henry is, tell me," Barry said with a slight smile.

"I don't know where he is, and even if I did, I wouldn't tell you," Jimmy snarled.

"Oh, but I think you will. The only reason you're still alive right now is because I believe I need you. Once that need is over, you can join your friend Jeffrey in the stew pot."

"What? What the hell are you talking about?" Jimmy snapped.

"Perhaps if you spend some time with your fellow captives you will change your mind." Barry looked to Keith. "Keith, please ungag the two ladies. Maybe after the young man has heard what they have to say, he'll change his mind." Then Barry walked out of the walk-in.

Keith walked over to Mary and Cindy and yanked off their gags without a care for his captive's welfare. He paused in front of Mary. His hand reached down and cupped her left breast and started to squeeze it gently. Mary struggled harder with her bonds, but it was hopeless. She was helpless to stop the man's advances. The sweat dripped down her back and became cold from the low temperature of the walk-in; the sweat feeling like ice water on her skin.

Jimmy saw what was happening and yelled at the bearded man.

"Get your goddamn hand off her, you fuckin' pervert."

Keith stopped what he was doing and moved back to Jimmy. With his right hand curled into a fist, he punched Jimmy in the jaw. Jimmy's head rocked back with the force of the blow and his vision faded for a moment. His head sagged down while he tried to recover.

Keith moved back to Mary and was about to continue when Mary spit into the man's right eye. The spittle ran down his cheek and landed on his boot.

With a snarl of rage, Keith raised his hand to slap Mary across the face.

She closed her eyes and waited for the blow, but it never came. Before the bearded man struck her, Barry's voice floated in from outside the door.

"Keith, where are you? I need you."

Keith dropped his hand and turned to leave, but before he left, he looked at Mary and smiled ruefully.

"I owe you for that bitch and I intend to collect later." Then he turned and exited the walk-in, closing the door behind him.

Both Mary and Cindy were relieved to see the man had left the light on.

As soon as the door was shut, Jimmy looked at the two women. He was still a little groggy from the punch, but he was feeling better with every second.

"What the hell is going on around here? I thought these guys were supposed to be our friends? Or at least allies," Jimmy asked the two women. "I mean, Henry told us what happened last night but this?"

Mary started to tell Jimmy what had happened to her and Cindy. Her voice cracked when she came to the part about Jeffrey, so Cindy had to finish the story.

Cindy told Jimmy how Jeffrey had been slaughtered and had then been taken out like a piece of meat.

"Then we sat in the dark for what seemed like hours, and that's when they brought you in," Cindy finished.

Jimmy sat quietly in his chair, too stunned to talk. Slowly it sank in and he looked at Mary.

"Good God, they're cannibals? Oh man, that ain't right. Well, look, at least Henry's still out there. Once he knows where we are, he'll come get us, but we can't wait for him. We have to assume we're on our own.

Jimmy's eyes scanned the walk-in. There was nothing in it but the three of them and the table used for slaughtering people like cattle. The table was rounded and smooth, no sharp edges on it to cut the ropes holding them captive.

Jimmy wracked his brain trying to think of a way out of their predicament. His hunting knife was missing, the empty sheath still strapped to his belt. He sat there for a few more minutes, the women talking quietly to each other, relieved not to be gagged anymore.

Then he realized something.

When he'd been searched, the guards had missed something. Jimmy looked up at the women and smiled, his grin going from ear to ear.

He just stared at them, his smile never faltering.

Cindy was the first to speak. "Maybe that guy hit him to hard and he's gone loopy," she suggested to Mary.

"Jimmy, what the hell are you smiling about?" Mary asked.

"I'm smiling because I just figured out how we're gonna get out of here," he said.

A few seconds passed and finally Mary spoke up.

"Yeah, well, tell us?" Mary requested frantically.

Jimmy held up his right boot. "Earlier today I found a Swiss Army knife. I stuck it in my sock. It's still there. They didn't find it. Shit, I forgot I had it," he beamed.

Both Mary and Cindy smiled, too, then.

"Jimmy when we get out of here, I'm gonna screw your brains out," Cindy said.

"I'm gonna hold you to that, babe," he said. He started to scoot his chair closer to Mary. Hopefully, with a little luck, he could get his leg up and Mary could reach in his sock and grab the small knife, then, with her hands bound, somehow pry the blade from its holder. Jimmy knew from experience how hard it could be to get the blade out when your hands were free. So now it could prove even more difficult. Plus, they had no idea when Barry or Keith might return. So they had to move fast.

With Jimmy sliding across the floor, and Mary stretching her hands, they began the arduous task of gaining their freedom.

CHAPTER TWENTY-FOUR

HENRY BLEW DUST from his face as he crawled through the ductwork of the shopping mall. Behind him were Jimmy's backpack and his shotgun. The rest was either on the floor or still in the ceiling above his sleeping quarters.

He stopped for a moment to catch his breath. His side ached where Vinnie had punched him and his wrist sent spasms of pain from where the noose had cut into his flesh. But that was okay. Better his wrist than his neck, he thought.

Crawling for another ten minutes, he came upon a four way intersection. The duct also went straight up, giving him a chance to sit up and stretch his back. The cramped confines of the ductwork were overbearing and it was only his shear will that was keeping him calm. While he wasn't claustrophobic, just being stuck inside the cramped space with no light was enough to freak anyone out.

Reaching into Jimmy's backpack by feel alone, he pulled out the box of shells for the shotgun. Jimmy's shotgun was still back in the ceiling with a full load of shells, but in the chaos to escape, he had grabbed his instead.

Carefully, by tactile sense alone, he loaded the barrel of the weapon. Once finished, he racked the pump, sending the first shell into the battery.

Now he was ready for what came next.

Lying back down, he started crawling again. His knees and elbows ached from the pressure being put on them, but it couldn't be helped. Soon, he rounded a corner and heard voices. Coming to a vent on the side of the duct, he slowed and shimmied the last few feet to the opening. There was a mesh of squares covering the vent and Henry was able to see down into the room it overlooked. He was looking at the living quarters of a family. They were talking about their children and the day to day things people chat about in their daily lives. Henry looked past them and was able to see the hallway of the mall. The store signs on the other side of the hallway were plainly visible and by using those, Henry was able to get his bearings. He continued onward. If the duct continued straight, then he would reach the food court in a half hour or so.

With a sigh, he started forward again, his clothes picking up the stray dust in the ducts until he was covered in a black mess of filth and debris.

He knew he was getting close to the kitchens when the odor of food cooking floated to his nose. Crawling a little faster, he soon came upon another metal-mesh vent cover. He looked down at what was once an Asian restaurant in the food court. The woks were all being used at the moment, the gas stoves jury-rigged to use propane or wood. Thick pieces of meat were being fried up in the woks and the rich smell of spices floated into the vent, causing Henry's stomach to rumble.

Four men worked over their pans of food, their weapons openly strapped to their hips. Unfortunately, he didn't know if the cooks were friend or foe.

Deciding this wouldn't be a good place to exit the ductwork, he continued onward. Soon, he heard more voices and the sound of a heavy cleaver as it chopped into meat. Cold air blew into the duct and Henry wondered how that could be.

Pulling himself up to the next vent, he looked down at the slaughterhouse from Hell.

The body of a dead man was lying on a large butcher block in a walk-in refrigerator. The arms and legs had already been removed and the two butchers were now cutting slabs of meat from the torso. But it was when Henry saw the head of the body that he felt his world fall apart.

It was Jeffrey.

Jeffrey's neck had been sliced open, the cut easy for Henry to see from his vantage point. Off to the side of the table was a large pot where the two butchers were placing the meat. Henry looked over the table and saw a pile of other heads sitting on a cart in the corner of the room. Men and women's faces looked out at nothing, the mouths curled up in frozen rictus' of death. Torsos hung from hooks suspended from the ceiling, small circles of blood pooling beneath each one.

Henry lay inside the duct and watched the two butchers work for another fifteen minutes, his mind still finding it hard to wrap itself around the visceral scene in front of him.

Then, one of the butchers went to the top of the table where Jeffrey lay.

Raising the butcher knife high in the air, he brought it down over Jeffrey's neck. Muscle and spine were severed in one cut, the head rolling to the side. Jeffrey's eyes were still open, the glazed orbs staring into nothing. The butcher picked up Jeffrey's head by the hair and tossed it onto the pile with the other severed heads. The head teetered for a moment and then settled down; one more hellish ornament in this shop of horrors.

The anger inside Henry continued to grow as his friend was cut up like a piece of Grade A meat. Finally, the rage had to come out. With a snarl, Henry reached down and grabbed his Glock. He still had more than half a clip left, and as the two men in the bloody aprons turned at the sound of Henry's screams, he knocked the vent open with the butt of his weapon.

The two men looked up, startled at the filthy man before them. Before either one could do more than gasp, Henry sent a round into the first butcher's temple. The man's head was thrown back and he slumped to the floor, dead; brains and bone splattering the stainless steel wall behind him.

The second man came alive. He ran at Henry, butcher knife in hand and tried to swipe at Henry's exposed arm, which was now sticking out of the vent.

Henry squeezed off a shot, but it just grazed the butcher's shoulder, the man barely noticing in his attack.

He continued charging forward with a snarl.

Henry quickly pulled his arm back, the cleaver striking sparks from the metal of the vent where it rebounded. The second the cleaver missed, Henry lined up the butcher again. This time his aim was true.

The .45 round hit the man in the chest, pulverizing his heart and exiting out the back. The butcher stumbled about the room for a few seconds while his synapses shut down.

Henry became tired of waiting for the man to die and shot him in the face. The second bullet struck the butcher in the middle of his shocked visage, destroying his nose and half of his cheek in a spray of blood and gore. The butcher dropped to the already bloody floor; dead before his body was fully prone.

Henry didn't care, he knew he had wasted a bullet, but that was fine. If he could have, he would have revived the bastard just so he could kill him again.

The smell of burnt meat and blood filled the room, making Henry retch slightly.

Swallowing the bile in his throat, he glanced one more time at Jeffrey's head and then pulled the vent closed. The latch was warped thanks to the butcher's attack, but he still managed to wedge it into place.

With any luck, by the time anyone figured out what had happened, it would be too late to sound the alarm.

With a grunt of aching limbs, Henry continued onward.

Someone was going to pay dearly for what he'd just discovered.

And he knew where to find him.

CHAPTER TWENTY-FIVE

THE SWISS KNIFE fell from Mary's frigid fingers for the fifth time.

"Damn it, Mary. You need to keep hold of it. Those bastards will probably be back any second."

"I'm trying," she screamed. "Jesus, Jimmy, I can barely feel my hands as it is."

Mary had been tied up for hours now, her hands numb from both the cold and her bonds.

Jimmy used his boots to collect the knife and bring it back up to Mary's hands.

"All right, I'm sorry. Let's try it again," Jimmy said.

"Can I try? I don't think the rope is as tight as it is on you, Mary. Maybe I might have better luck," Cindy suggested.

Mary slumped in her chair as she looked at Jimmy. "She's got a point. I can't feel my fingertips as it is. Give me the knife and I'll pass it to her," Mary told him.

Jimmy nodded. "Okay, here goes." He lifted his boots up so they were only an inch from Mary's tied hands. Mary could only go by touch, her hands bound behind her back. Finally, she managed to grasp the cold metal in her numb fingers. Jimmy dropped his boots to the floor with a loud thump.

"There, that's good. Now, Cindy, can you spin around in your chair and get the knife from her?" Jimmy asked.

Cindy nodded quickly and began to push with her feet. The metal chair legs scraped long scratches in the metal floor as she slowly moved around behind Mary.

After five long minutes, she made it and reached out to touch Mary's fingers. By using just her fingertips, she felt the cold metal of the knife. Using her first two fingers of her right hand, she managed to pluck the blade from Mary's hand. Then she carefully used the nail of her thumb to pry open the blade. She could feel her nail separating from her finger, but still she pushed and pried. Just before the nail was completely ripped free, the blade popped out.

From where Jimmy sat, he was able to see her working at it.

Now he yelled with glee. "You did it! Holy shit, I don't believe it!"

Cindy frowned. "Thanks for the vote of confidence," she said as she looked to Mary. "Come a little closer, Mary, and I'll cut you free first, then once you're free you can do us."

Mary answered by pushing back the few inches Cindy needed. Cindy started cutting, although because of the position and lack of sight, she frequently cut into Mary's hand and wrists. Mary would yelp each time the blade would slice her flesh, the thin cuts stinging.

"Sorry, Mary, I can't see what I'm doing," Cindy said.

Mary ignored her. "Forget it, just get me free and all is forgiven," she said.

Three minutes later, Mary pulled apart her cut bonds, the bloody ropes falling to the floor. Ignoring her bleeding, stinging wounds, she quickly cut Jimmy loose and then went to work on Cindy.

One minute later, all three were free and standing in the walk-in, rubbing their wrists. Mary picked up a rag in the corner and wrapped it around her cut right hand; the left one only had some superficial cuts, little more than bad paper cuts. The three friends looked at each other.

"Well, we may be out of our chairs, but we're still stuck in here," Jimmy said.

"Then let's go!" Cindy said, moving for the door.

"No wait!" Mary yelled. "We don't know what's on the other side of that door. If we open it and Barry or a guard is out there, then we're caught before we can go two feet. I have a better idea."

Jimmy and Cindy moved closer to her and Mary filled them in on her idea. It was risky, but they didn't have a lot of options.

While the three stood there shivering in the middle of the walk-in huddling together for warmth, Mary filled them in on her plan.

*   *   *

Henry had come to the end of the duct system.

The end turned out to be a long drop straight down deep into the building, where he assumed it finished up in the basement. He had no room to turn around, and so had to slowly back up again, until he came to the most recent meshed vent cover he'd passed earlier.

The oppressiveness of the duct was overwhelming and sweat began to bead on his brow. He tried to wipe it with his shirt sleeve and only managed to cover his face with more dirt and grime.

Ten agonizing minutes later he passed the vent he was looking for. After taking a quick look to see that the room was clear, he knocked the mesh cover open with the butt of his Glock.

Climbing out head first, he tumbled out and fell the five feet to the carpeted floor. He tucked his head to his chest to hopefully prevent himself from a snapped neck, and his boots dropped hard to the floor. His breath flew out of him and he saw stars for a moment as he lay prone on the carpet in a heap of arms and legs.

After a full two minutes had passed, he blinked the dust from his eyes and rolled to a more dignified position.

His Glock had fallen from his hand and he reached over and picked it up. When he was able, he stood up, and after a slight wave of dizziness came and went, he walked around his new environment.

He was in an office, the computer and the paperwork on the desk in the corner showing the room hadn't been used for quite a while.

Looking up at the ceiling, he noticed the same skylight architecture as in Barry's office. The sun was starting to go down, the short November night already making itself known.

He pulled the .357 from his back and checked it. With the exception of some of his skin catching in the trigger, the weapon seemed sound. He grabbed a chair and then used it to reach back up into the vent. Finding what he wanted, he pulled out his shotgun and the backpack. Feeling as ready as he thought he could be, given the circumstances, he went to the only door in the room.

Opening it a crack, he saw a long hallway similar to the one that led to Barry's office. The hallway was empty. Slowly and quietly, he stepped out into the hallway and closed the door behind him. He hated feeling so exposed, but it couldn't be helped.

Making his way to the end, he stopped at a long stairwell leading down. Voices floated up to him and he listened for a moment. He distinctly heard his name spoken as well as Keith's.

So there were guards down below.

He wondered if anyone had found the two men in the giant refrigerator yet. Once they were found, he knew the entire complex would be up in arms.

If it wasn't already.

With his Glock leading the way, he crept his way down the stairs, careful not to let the shotgun hit the railing, where it hung from his shoulder on its leather strap.

He slid down the wall until he came to another door. This one was open an inch and the voices he had heard seconds ago filtered through from the other side.

Peeking through the crack in the door, he could see two silhouettes framed in the dim light of the hallway only a foot from the door. It was apparent to Henry the men were on watch, but for what was a mystery.

Were they waiting for him or something else?

Their backs were to the door; evidently they weren't worried about being attacked from the rear. That would be a mistake they would pay for, Henry thought.

Henry pressed his boot against the door and pushed with all of his 190 plus pounds of solid muscle. The man closest to the door went flying across the hall, his rifle sliding on the floor. The second man stood with his mouth open. Henry looked like something that had come up from the depths of Hell. His clothes were covered in soot and dust; his frame blending in with the shadows of the opening. His face was streaked with dirt, making him look like he was ready to tackle the jungles of Vietnam instead of the guards in the shopping mall.

For a split second all was silent as the two guards stared at the demon in front of them. Henry's voice was filled with ice as he leveled the Glock at both men. "Freeze! You move, you die!" Henry yelled.

Neither listened, both reaching for their weapons at the same time.

"Fair enough," he growled.

Henry took out the guard still standing upright first as the man leveled his rifle at Henry.

Henry squeezed the trigger twice in quick succession and the rounds hammered the guard in the chest and neck, sending the dying man flying back to hit the far wall. In the confines of the small stone hallway, the gunshots sounded like cannon shots; the blasts echoing off the cement walls.

Realizing his rifle was out of reach, the second guard pulled a knife and lunged at Henry's legs. Henry kicked out with his boot, the tip catching the man in the chin. His head was knocked back and the man rolled away. A second later, the guard shook it off, adrenalin feeding his attack. He lunged again and Henry aimed and fired at the man, going for the side of his chest. But the bullet only grazed the guard's shoulder. The guard shrugged it off and lunged again.

Cursing his luck, Henry put two more rounds into the man's neck and head.

The guard dropped to the floor, the upper half of his body nothing but a red ruin, a vermilion puddle spreading out below the prone body.

Henry stopped and listened for sounds of reinforcements, but nothing floated to his ears. Satisfied he was safe for the moment; he bent over and retrieved the man's knife. It was a seven inch hunting knife and could come in handy later. Retrieving the sheath and sliding the knife into his boot, he headed off down the hallway. He'd kill every guard in this place until he found his friends. If it wasn't for all the innocent people living inside the shopping mall, he would have opened it to the undead horde outside and let the dead have free reign.

Instead, he had to do it quietly, only taking out specific targets. But that was okay with him. He'd learned a lot since he had killed his first ghoul all those months ago.

Since then he had hardened into a warrior, who would show mercy when necessary, but would take a life if he had to.

With his jaw set in stone, he moved off down the hallway…to find more targets.

CHAPTER TWENTY-SIX

JIMMY, MARY AND CINDY waited by the walk-in door for someone to return. Minutes passed, and before they knew it, over an hour had gone by.

Jimmy looked to Mary, his teeth chattering.

"Mary, I don't know how much more of this I can take. It's freezing in here."

Mary scrunched up her nose in disgust at his statement. "Oh, give me a break. Cindy and I have been in here for a hell of a lot longer than you and you don't see us complaining," she said.

Cindy had her head down against her chest. She was exhausted and had nodded off for a few minutes.

Hearing her name, she perked back up. "What? Did someone say my name?" The blonde girl asked.

Mary turned to her and placed her hand on her shoulder. "No, honey, I'm sorry, I was talking to your macho boyfriend, here."

"Hey, just because I'm cold doesn't mean I'm not a man," he said.

Mary smiled at him. "Relax, tough guy, I'm just joking."

The handle to the refrigerator door started to jiggle as pressure was added from the other side.

Someone was coming in.

"Okay, someone's here, its show time," Mary said.

All three companions placed their hands behind their backs and quickly sat back down. From the door it would look like they were still tied up. The door opened and Keith stepped inside, stopping at the opening. Behind him were two more guards. Although they had rifles over their shoulders, the two men acted like the companions were absolutely no threat.

And why should they?

The three people had been locked in a refrigerated room for more than a few hours and were tied up. They were harmless.

Keith smiled, crossing his arms over his chest. "Ready to talk? If you're not, I have a present for you," he said while reaching behind his back. He pulled Jimmy's hunting knife out. "I thought it would be poetic if I killed you with your own knife," he said while staring at Jimmy. "And when I'm finished with you, I'll have some fun with her," he said, leering at Mary. "And then I'll let my guards have the blonde."

"Screw you, asshole," Jimmy said. Pretending he was trying to get loose of his bonds.

Keith sneered. "I'm gonna enjoy this," he said, moving closer to Jimmy.

Mary was now directly on Keith's left, the man ignoring her again. Mary jumped up and kicked the man in his left leg. The leg crumpled from the force of the blow, the bearded man falling to the floor. But he never made it that far. As soon as Mary struck, Jimmy was up and out of his chair. He sent his leg into Keith's kidneys, the blow pushing the air from his lungs. Jimmy kept moving, throwing punches, he owed this man and it was time to make him pay. No sooner had his right fist connected with Keith's face, then Jimmy's left fist was striking his stomach. And, he wasn't through with the man yet. Jimmy swung back his right leg again and with all his weight behind it, sent it streaking up to connect to the man's groin. Keith's testicles were crushed and the man fell over to the floor, curling up in a ball from the excruciating pain.

While this was happening, Mary and Cindy had attacked the two guards at the opening to the walk-in refrigerator.

Right after Mary had kicked Keith in the leg; she picked up her chair and charged at the two guards with Cindy right behind her. Caught unaware and shocked to see the tied up captives charging at them waving a chair, the two men quickly tried to unshoulder their rifles. But it was too little, too late.

Mary burst through the door and struck the first guard in the forehead with the chair, the metal rattling from the force of the blow.

Skin split and blood started to flow into the man's eyes as he struggled to bring his weapon around, screaming in pain and fear. Cindy had run past Mary and had tackled the other guard, knocking him to the floor. Her hand shot out and struck the man in his trachea, shattering cartilage. The man gasped for breath on the floor of the outer room, but Cindy was still moving. There was a video monitor sitting on a desk, now useless in the new world, but Cindy picked it up and held it over her head, her arms straining from the weight.

The man's eyes pleaded for mercy and she almost stopped, but then she thought of Jeffrey, killed like an animal and then brought down to the kitchens. The fire flared back inside her and she brought the monitor down onto the guard's head. The glass shattered, blood running across the floor. The man's limbs twitched in his death throes; then mercifully, they stopped.

Cindy turned to see if Mary needed help, but it wasn't necessary. The other guard was down, unconscious. His skull was bleeding heavily like only a head wound could. Cindy looked at Mary and Mary looked back, breathing heavily from the exertion.

She shook her head. "I'm not going to kill him. He's out of it. Even if he gets help, he won't be a threat to us. Lets just lock him in there," she said, pointing over her shoulder to the walk-in fridge.

Jimmy walked out of the room and closed the door behind him. His fists were covered in blood as well as his right boot. The women looked at him and he smiled wanly. He held up both his knife and his recovered .38.

"Look what I found," he said.

The women walked over to the desk and sat down. They were exhausted. Their skin tingled with the returning warmth from the room they were now in. It felt great after being cold for so long.

Cindy looked at Jimmy. "What about Keith?"

Jimmy shook his head. "Dead," he said, crouching beside the prone guard.

Mary turned to Jimmy who was inspecting the unconscious guard. "So what's next?" Mary asked.

Jimmy looked up at the two women. "First we get their rifles and see how much ammo we have. Second, we find Barry and kill him, and third, we find Henry and get the hell out of here."

Mary slid off the desk, her footing a little unsteady for a moment.

God she wished she could just lay down and take a nap, she thought.

Then she bent over and retrieved the rifles. Handing one to Cindy, she stood back up, her back showing its discomfort. Then she reopened the walk-in and dragged the unconscious guard inside, a trail of red remaining on the vinyl tiled floor.

Her face was ashen when she exited the walk-in, the sight of what Jimmy had done to Keith still etched on her eyes. Jimmy saw the look she wore and he shrugged casually.

"The prick deserved every second of it, Mary. I just wished he would have lasted longer."

She only nodded and pushed the door closed, sliding the pin through the lock. Jimmy was right, of course. The coldheart would have done far worse to them all if given the chance. Jimmy just had been first to the punch.

The three companions got down to business, checking weapons and getting ready to venture outside. They didn't know what waited for them, but Henry was out there and he would probably need help.

And the sooner he received it the better.

CHAPTER TWENTY-SEVEN

HENRY OPENED THE door at the end of the hallway he was in.

Looking through the crack in the door, he saw he was directly adjacent to the food court.

He watched while the residents ate their supper, some with their children with them.

He needed to make a decision. Did he want to backtrack and climb back into the claustrophobic ventilation system? Or did he want to take his chances in the food court.

As he watched the residents moving about, he noticed only three guards scattered around the food court. They walked around casually, chatting with people whenever they were near.

He didn't want to have a gunfight in the middle of all those innocents, not if he could help it.

Then, from across the court, he saw Barry walking. The man was with only one guard, and as Henry watched, Barry stopped and shook a few residents' hands.

He ground his teeth together while he watched the leader of the mall. If these people only knew what a monster they had for a leader, they would probably turn on him themselves. But there was no way to get the truth out in time.

Then he spotted Gwen moving through the crowd, but she was not coming anywhere near him.

Cursing under his breath, he made his decision.

He would move quickly and keep to the corners of the food court, and with any luck, he would make it to the end and disappear down one of the many hallways. Then, if he was spotted, he could take out the guard's that pursued him without fear of any of the residents becoming caught in the crossfire.

Barry disappeared behind the fire door leading to his office. That was where Henry really wanted to go, but he didn't see how without causing a commotion. The area between him and the stairwell was wide open and he would be spotted as soon as he stepped through the door he was hiding behind.

With a weary sigh, he waited for the right time to move.

The minutes ticked by and Henry watched and waited until it seemed most of the diners had either left or were occupied.

When he saw his chance, he sucked in a deep breath, said a silent prayer for luck, and slipped out of the door into the shadows of the food court. Moving from column to column, he had thought he'd made it when a shout rang out across the open area. A reckless guard fired at him, the stray round chipping a piece of tile a foot from his head. Ducking and cursing, he kept moving. Another shot rang out and a piece of the floor bit into his leg from the ricochet. He raised his Glock and sent two rounds high and wide, hoping to gain a few precious seconds.

It worked, the guard ducking behind a column for cover.

Then he was around the corner and running down the hallway. As he ran, he passed blurred faces that looked up quickly and caught a glimpse of him as he shot by. Through screams of surprise and terror, he kept moving.

He soon realized where he was and made a sharp turn down another hallway.

Five store fronts down on the left were where Gwen's school and sleeping quarters were located. With a quick look around to see if anyone was watching, he dived inside the room. Moving to the back, he hid behind a pile of boxes, the Glock aimed at the opening leading to the hallway.

A minute later he heard voices as the following guards and a few residents ran by him. Then the voices faded away as they continued deeper into the shopping mall.

Henry breathed a deep sigh of relief.

For the immediate moment, he was safe. Now all he had to do was find his friends while evading the growing search parties.

Half an hour later, noises floated from the front of the large room. Henry was startled from a light doze, the exertions of the day and the receding adrenalin making him weary. Deciding he should sleep if he had the chance, he had welcomed it. But now there was someone out front. He could hear things being move around. It was completely dark, he noticed, the sun having set on another day. The slight illumination from a single candle cast flickering shadows across the room. He stayed where he was, patiently waiting for the person in front to give some sign if they were friend or foe.

Then the noise stopped.

Henry decided he would have to take the initiative and he slowly crawled out from behind the boxes and peeked out front. From where he stood, the blackboard was blocking his view.

Cursing his luck, he moved closer. As he approached his target, he heard the slight ruffle of pages of a book being turned. Slowly, he moved forward until he was directly behind the blackboard. Moving to the side, he was going to have to jump out and then pull his opponent to the floor.

Taking a quick deep breath to prepare himself, he lunged out from behind his cover and reached out to grab his opponent.

A woman turned around quickly, hearing the sound of someone behind her. Henry stopped himself and found himself looking into the frightened eyes of Gwen.

"Oh my God, Henry, you scared me half to death! What are you doing here? Do you know that every security guard Barry has is out looking for you?"

Henry looked down at her, and nodded. "Yeah, I know. And I think you want to know why they're after me, too. I found out where all your missing people have gone to."

Gwen's eyebrows went up in a questioning look. "And?"

Someone walked by the hallway outside. "Wait, first let's get under cover. I don't want anyone seeing me," he said.

She stared at him for a second and then her eyes lit up with understanding. "Oh, of course, how stupid of me. Come on, we can go into the back. I believe you know the way?" She joked.

Henry glanced back at her and saw the slight smile crease her face. He liked that smile. Then they moved to the back. Once there, he filled her in on the butchery of the missing residents and the pile of heads he had seen in the corner of the room.

She nodded at his story, and despite being clearly horrified, she was keeping a level head.

"That explains a lot. Especially about what happened when we were desperately low on food. One day Barry miraculously said he'd found meat for us. Everyone was so hungry no one thought to question him. From that day on, he was the mall's savior; even more so than before. But now it all makes sense. That bastard, he has to pay."

Henry nodded. "And I intend to make him, but I could use some help."

Her eyes opened wide. "Really, what can I do?"

"Well, for starters, you can tell me the quickest way to get to the roof."

"The roof, but why?" She asked, curious.

Henry smiled, his teeth flashing in the gloom of the backroom.

"Let's just say I need a distraction. But to make sure no one gets hurt with the exception of Barry and his guards I'll need your help. Are you in?"

Gwen looked at Henry with a look that reminded him of Mary. "You bet your ass I'm in, just tell me what you want me to do."

"Later, right now I'm starving, I haven't eaten all day, besides I won't need to be on the roof until the morning foraging team goes out. Can you find out when that is?"

She nodded. "I think so. I'll check while I get you some food. I'll tell a few of my friends about what's happened, too. They'll need to know what's really been going on."

"Good idea," Henry grunted, "but about the food, just make sure it doesn't have any meat in it."

Turning to look at him, she frowned. "I don't know whether to laugh or be mad at you for that statement."

"Yeah, I know what you mean, make it the former, okay?"

She gazed at him for another heartbeat, her expression neutral. Then she waved and disappeared to find him some food.

Henry sat down to wait for Gwen to return.

While the mall settled down for another night, he went over the plan in his head to take down Barry.

Chapter Twenty-eight

Jimmy, Mary and Cindy were hiding out in a backroom of one of the vacant stores. At the moment, however, none of them was quite sure what they should do.

"First we need to find Henry. If they had grabbed him or worse, killed him, we would have heard about it from Keith, that bastard would have loved to gloat about that," Jimmy said.

Mary nodded in agreement. "True, but how do we find him? We may be armed, but it's not that much compared to the security force out there. Yesterday at dinner, I remember Barry saying something about over twenty men being on the force. We've only killed a couple, that's still way too many for just us to take on alone."

"We should just sneak out of here. Maybe hook up with Henry later?" Cindy suggested. At the moment she was curled up next to Jimmy, the two not leaving each other's side since they had left the refrigerator.

Jimmy shook his head. "Too risky, besides, once we leave this mall we have to deal with hundreds of rotters."

Mary made a face. "Don't call them that, Jimmy. I don't like it."

"Sorry Mar', you know, when in Rome and all that shit."

Cindy yawned and stretched her shapely legs. The day had been unbelievable. She still couldn't believe they had escaped in one piece.

Mary saw her yawn and she caught it, yawning, too. Then Jimmy started.

"Will you guys cut it out, it's contagious, you know," Jimmy said, finishing his yawn.

Mary looked around the backroom where they were hiding. "Listen, we're all exhausted. Why don't we stay here for the night and we'll start fresh tomorrow. Maybe by then we'll know where Henry is. If I know the man, he won't stay hidden for long."

Jimmy rubbed his chin, feeling the stubble accumulating there. "You think he's gonna cause some trouble?" Jimmy asked.

Mary looked Jimmy straight in the eyes. "We are talking about the same man, right?"

"Yeah, good point," he agreed and stretched his legs. The blood on his boot had started to dry to a brown crust and flakes would fall off whenever his foot hit the floor. "All right then, let's sleep," he said

The room was already dark, the few windows set in the wall too high to reach, and with the darkness outside, the light was almost nonexistent.

Using what they could find in the storeroom, they made some makeshift bedrolls and then jammed the door shut. No one would be surprising them in the middle of the night. The three survivors stretched out and let sleep take them.

Each one drifted off within minutes, despite the early hour. The darkness and their own exhaustion more than enough to knock them out.

Outside in the hallways of the mall complex the security force of the Crystal Mall continued the search for the outsiders.

* * *

After Henry finished eating a meager meal of crackers and old cheese, he lay back and stretched his tired bones.

Next to him, Gwen sat on a stool. He looked up at her as he lay on the floor.

"You know, the first time I saw you, I could have sworn you were my wife."

Her eyebrows went up in understanding. Henry was starting to like that about her. An amusing trait she did often.

"Oh, really? And what happened when you saw it was just little ole me?"

"At first I was disappointed, but after a moment or so, I was glad it was you. From that second on I hoped I'd get to meet you."

"Really, why Mr. Watson, I do believe you're making a pass at me."

"And if I was?"

She thought for a moment, the corner of her mouth going up in a crooked grin.

"If you were, I do believe I'd let you."

He smiled at that. Then he held out his hand to her. She looked at it for another heartbeat, and then she reached out with her own and took it.

With a gentle pull, Henry pulled her to him. With a small utterance of surprise, she fell into his arms. Both of them sat quite still, staring into each others eyes. Then Henry leaned forward just a little, seeing what she'd do.

Gwen leaned forward just a hint as well. Their mouths were only a few inches from each other and Henry's heart beat just a little faster in his chest.

He leaned forward a little more and she did the same. Henry decided it was now or never and he pressed his lips to hers. The sensation was cool and warm at the same time. Lips met and tongues mingled gently.

She pulled away. Her eyes had tears in them.

"I haven't been with another man since my husband died," she said, her breath coming in excited gasps.

He shook his head. "Me neither. Until this moment, I didn't want to be with another woman, either."

"And that's changed?" She breathed softly.

He nodded. "Oh, yes. As of right now, everything's changed."

She smiled and leaned back into him. They kissed again, softly and as their passion grew, so did their kisses become more animated. Before either of them realized, clothes were coming off and they were making love. Henry would frequently have to change his body's position thanks to the beating he had suffered from Vinnie, but they managed.

Hands began to explore one another, her pale skin a sharp contrast to his tanned body.

Henry slowly ran his hand down the nape of her neck, caressing her nipples gently, then he slid his calloused hand into the warmness between her thighs. She uttered a hesitant breath and he paused for a fraction of a second. He separated his lips from hers and looked into her eyes. She nodded that she was fine and with a soft nuzzle, he began kissing her again, while his hand began to make circling motions between her thighs. She moaned in pleasure, and before she realized it, she was shaking all over, a warm fuzziness filling her inside.

With her chuckling like a school girl with embarrassment, Henry took his hand away, then began softly caressing her nipples with his mouth.

She moaned in ecstasy, and when he was ready, he gently climbed on top of her. He gazed into her eyes and she nodded, signifying she was ready by spreading her legs wide. Reaching down to his manhood, she stroked him gently, then helped him into position.

When he thrust into her warmness, she shuddered in response, the two lovers becoming one person as they lost themselves in the fulfillment of life itself.

Gwen gasped in pleasure, her nails clawing his back in sweet happiness. Henry continued plunging into her, the feeling indescribable.

Emily floated to the forefront of his mind and he pushed it away. He had mourned for long enough, it was time to live again, though he still loved his late wife dearly.

Gwen's eyes were open, and she gazed into his hard eyes, a few tears slipping from her lids as she slowly reached orgasm. As Henry rose and fell with a steady rhythm, she began to meet his thrusts, arching her back as she hovered on the edge of exploding.

Soft words were exchanged, sweet nothings as two people joined as one, and Henry felt himself close to the breaking point.

Soon words were stopped and only their breathing filled their ears. Thrusting, grinding, eyes closed in ecstasy, suddenly Henry felt himself release, as Gwen shook with pleasure beneath him. The two continued to move as one, the sweet perfection of pure bliss filling both their souls in an overwhelming exchange of emotion.

Then he collapsed on top of her and she wrapped her arms and legs around his muscled body, kissing his neck as her heartbeat slowed to a more manageable level, their sweat-slicked bodies sliding against one another.

After a few seconds, Henry rolled off her and the two became entangled in each other limbs as they relished the fading glow of their passion.

Neither spoke, as there was nothing that needed to be said.

When two hearts became one, speech was meaningless.

Fifteen minutes later they were resting, curled up in each others arms and Henry finally broke the silence.

"You know this won't last. Once I'm through here, I'll be moving on," Henry said.

Nodding slightly, she curled up closer to him. "I know, but until then, let's just think about the here and now."

He looked down at her face, only the shadows of her features could be seen in the darkened room.

"Mrs. Willis, that seems like an excellent idea. Ready for round two?"

She giggled and climbed on top of him for an answer.

The rest of the night was spent making love and sleeping.

While the world may have gone to Hell outside the walls of the shopping mall, to Henry, with Gwen lying next to him, he felt like he was in Heaven.

CHAPTER TWENTY-NINE

THE NEXT MORNING Henry made his way to the roof.

Thanks to Gwen's help, he was able to bypass any security and made it to the roof unopposed.

The sun was still rising in the sky, the clear-blue horizon forecasting a pleasant day. There was a nip in the air, but otherwise it was comfortable.

Once Henry had made it to the roof, he had spotted the guard near the edge. Next to the man sat the pinger switch. Stealthily, he had crept as close as he dared, not wanting to commit to an attack just yet.

He needed to wait for just the right moment. The man needed to be taken down quickly and silently, before he could sound the alarm.

Outside, on the pavement below, in front of the loading dock's, bay metal doors, were hundreds of the undead. They knew there was meat inside the shopping mall and so stayed there twenty-four hours a day.

The smell was awful, the stench of rotting meat filling the air, causing his stomach to spin inside him. Then the breeze shifted and Henry caught a full whiff of the stench of death and he truly thought he was going to vomit.

Covering his nose with his shirt, he tried not to gag by will power alone and wondered how the man could stand it out here on the roof for hours on end.

The guard stood up and leaned over the side, wanting to survey the scene below. Leaning over the side of the roof, his attention was only focused forward while the man precariously balanced over the edge.

Deciding it was the best time to move, Henry crouched low, and when the man leaned over to spit off the edge, trying to hit the walking corpses below, Henry sprinted at the man. For the first few feet, Henry made it across unobserved, but then his boots crunching on the gravel floated to the guard's ears.

The guard looked up when Henry was only ten feet away. Panicking, the man dropped the box and tried to pick up his rifle, but it was already too late.

As the man brought the rifle up and tried to point it at his attacker, Henry slammed the stock of his shotgun into his forehead.

The guard dropped to the roof like he'd been slapped by a giant hand; unconscious before he hit the gravel. Before the guard could fall to the ghouls below, Henry grabbed his shirt and carefully laid him on the graveled roof. There was no way of knowing if this man was truly a threat or only following orders, so Henry decided to spare his life. Quickly, Henry ripped a piece of the unconscious man's shirt into ribbons with his panga and then secured his arms behind his back.

Once his arms and legs were secured, Henry dragged him across the roof and hid the unconscious body between a pair of air vents. The fans turned slightly in the wind, despite being non-functional without power.

Henry quickly darted back to the roof's edge, just in time to hear the two-way radio crackle to life. Bending over, he retrieved the radio and placed it to his ear.

"We're ready down here, turn on the pinger," the radio speaker said through bits of static.

"10-4," Henry said and then looked down at the shoebox like container. It was so simple it was ridiculous. There were two buttons, one for ON and one for Off. Henry pressed the ON button and immediately heard the sound of the pinger start. Looking over the edge, he watched the walking dead pause at the loading dock doors and then as one group, begin to shuffle away across the parking lot toward the distant pinging.

Henry waited as minutes passed. When the undead were no more than twenty-feet away, he pressed the Off button. The ghouls stopped and looked around stupidly. After only seconds, they turned and moved back to the loading dock doors. Just before the first corpse would have reached the bay doors, he switched the pinger back on. The ghouls stopped and then once again moved off toward the sound.

Henry did this for the next five minutes, keeping the animated corpses in a holding pattern in front of the bay doors. He knew from when he'd gone on the foraging trip that the men in the truck inside the loading dock expected to wait at least five minutes before receiving the all clear to open the doors.

Checking his watch, and satisfied the correct amount of time had elapsed, he called the all clear on the radio. The ghouls were about ten feet away from the loading doors. As the bay doors went up, the way looked clear. With the pinger off, the zombies started to swarm into the bay. The shocked men reached for their weapons, but it was already too late to close the doors again.

Within seconds, they were overwhelmed and pulled down to the cement floor. Their bodies were ripped apart as the ghouls feasted on their insides. One guard tried to lock himself inside the cab of the truck, but in less than a minute a dead man with half a face and a rock smashed in the glass. What seemed like a hundred hands reached for the screaming guard and pulled him through the opening. With his shrieks for help carrying in harmony with the moans of the undead, the man died in excruciating pain.

With all the guards dead, the ghouls continued to eat the remains, fighting over scraps of organs and bones.

Up on the roof, Henry smiled.

Now that was a distraction. Every guard in the shopping mall would be moving to the loading docks to contain the invasion. But if Gwen had done her job, then the mall would be safe.

Now he had to wait and let things play out.

* * *

Gwen stood in front of the door that separated the mall from the loading dock. A set of metal double doors in a solid metal frame stood open behind her, those leading to the mall itself.

Inside the loading dock, she could hear the men as they waited for the undead to evacuate from in front of the bay doors. The men had done this countless times and today was no different. They lounged around in the truck's bed or on the stairs leading down into the bays. An extra man stood by the chains that would open the large accordion-type doors. On his waist was a radio. The radio crackled with the all clear and the man started to pull on the chains. The doors slid up overhead on the ceiling tracks and the men in the truck prepared to leave.

Suddenly, a wall of rotting bodies started to flood into the docks. For a heartbeat, Gwen was stunned and almost didn't accomplish her assigned task, but she broke from her stupor and quickly pulled the double doors closed. She shot the bolts at the top and bottom of the door into the floor and ceiling and let out a small scream when a ghoul struck the door. Its rotting face left streaks of pus and blood on the reinforced glass in the middle of the door as it tried to get through. But she knew the mall was safe. As long as that door remained bolted, no one could get through, alive or dead.

"Well, well, what do we have here?" A voice said from the end of the hall.

Gwen recognized the voice even before she turned around. It was Barry, with two guards behind him.

"May I ask you what you're doing here?" Barry inquired pleasantly.

Gwen stood stock still, her eyes locked with Barry's.

Barry turned and looked through the glass at the carnage inside the loading dock. His mouth turned down into a grimace.

"You have something to do with this, yes? One of my guards saw you talking with Henry yesterday. I think you will stay with me until I sort out your involvement."

"I don't know what you're talking about. I heard screams and came to investigate," Gwen added with her chin held high.

"Oh really," Barry said.

"You want us to bring her to the kitchens, Boss?" One of the guards asked.

Gwen's eyes lit up with a fire she didn't realize she had in her.

"The kitchens? You bastard, how could you, we trusted you," she said to the leader of the shopping mall as Henry's story came to the forefront of her mind. Everything Henry had told her was true!

There was no doubt about it now. The guard's question had washed away any doubts she may have had.

Behind her, in the loading dock, the screams of the dying men permeated the metal door.

Barry walked closer to her while behind him the two guards stood with rifles pointed in her direction. She gulped silently, but tried to stand her ground.

"If you are talking about what I think you are, then may I inquire how you found out? I'd like to think I was discreet."

The anger in her was boiling over and she answered without thinking.

"Henry told me, he saw your entire twisted operation. What the hell is wrong with you? Killing and eating your own people? My God, that's sick."

Barry's eyes flared with anger. "Sick? What about when you were all starving? I didn't see anyone complaining then. No, I simply did what had to be done. So a few died, at least the rest of us are still here."

Gwen stared up at him defiantly. "That's bullshit and you know it. We could have started growing our own food. We could have found some animals out there and started to breed them. There are so many things we could have done, but you decided to indulge in your sick fantasies. But guess what, it ends here, Henry is going to shut you down."

Barry started to, laugh. "Oh, really? One man is going to stop me? I still have at least fifteen men. True, the man has caused me some damage, but he will be dealt with soon enough. As for you, my dear, you are a traitor. And when this is all over, I will make you pay for that treachery. When I am through with you, you will pray that I gave you to them." He said, pointing to the zombies banging on the glass of the metal door.

"You, give me your radio," Barry said to the nearest guard. The man did as requested and Barry placed the radio to his mouth.

"Attention, this is Barry. We have a breach at the loading docks. I want all available men to report there immediately. We need to keep the rotters contained." Barry then looked to Gwen, an unctuous sneer on his lips.

"For now, my dear, I think you can escort me. I don't have time to send you to the kitchens just now and you might prove useful. You, bring her with us," he ordered, pointing to the second guard. With a nod, the man grabbed Gwen's wrists. She fought for a moment and then realized she was no match for the large man holding her. She sagged in his arms.

Two more guards arrived and Barry called them to him. "All of you, follow me to the roof, the pinger is the only way we're going to get rid of those damn rotters. There must be something wrong up there." Then he headed off, with the four guards following, Gwen being dragged along in the middle.

Barry spotted another security guard and called to him. "Go and guard the loading dock doors, don't allow them to be opened for anything. Your life and ours depends on it."

The man nodded, and with a "yes, sir," ran off down the hallway.

Barry continued across the mall. He paused for just a moment and looked down the long hallway, wondering where Keith had gotten off to. With things escalating as they were, he needed him. Reaching the fire door leading to the roof, he pushed through and started up the stairs, the four guards and Gwen behind him.

Upon reaching the roof, he pushed open the access door and strode out into the light of the day. The six people moved across the gravel, their shoes and boots crunching as they walked. Upon reaching the edge, Barry looked down to the asphalt below. Dozens of zombies milled about the opening to the loading dock. Looking around the roof, he could see no sign of the spotter. That was odd, he thought, there was always a man on watch with the controls to the pinger.

Suddenly, a loud blast filled the air around him and the guard to his right was thrown off the roof like he'd been punched with a giant fist. The man tumbled head over heels until he landed head first on the pavement. His head imploded on impact, brains and skull fragments spinning across the asphalt. Immediately the undead swarmed over the body, tearing into it like locusts.

Another blast followed soon after the first and the guard to Barry's left fell to the roof with half his face missing. He screamed once and then his voice was gone as he dropped to the hard ground and ghouls below.

In shock at this sudden occurrence, Barry looked across the roof, not yet understanding what was happening. The other two guards had gone to cover behind some ductwork, Gwen forgotten for the moment.

She was about to run, when Barry locked his fingers around her left wrist and yanked her towards his chest.

"Not so fast, my dear, I believe you may still help me," he said. Wrapping his arm around her waist, he pulled a knife from his back pocket and held it to her throat.

"One move, my dear, and I'll cut your throat," he hissed into her ear. Barry looked around the roof, his eyes searching frantically.

"Where are you, you bastard? Come out or I'll kill her!" He yelled.

Henry stepped out onto the roof from behind an air conditioning unit.

"So kill her, what do I care?" He growled.

Barry laughed. "Oh, really. I don't believe you. If that was true then you would have shot me already. No, I think you like this one, eh?" He said, moving the tip of the blade across Gwen's cheek. Her eyes watched the blade and she let out a soft squeal. Henry's heart skipped a beat at seeing Gwen taken hostage, but he knew he needed to stay calm. If Barry thought he had the upper hand, he would never see this day through alive, or Gwen.

"What do you want?" Henry asked.

"I want you to drop your weapons so I can kill you," he stated almost casually. "You've caused me a great deal of trouble already, Watson. If Keith hadn't been such a coward, he would have killed you and your troublesome friends out on the road and none of this would be happening. And then you had to kill my second-hand man, Vinnie. Now he is going to be hard to replace."

"No deal," Henry growled. "How about I take the woman and I leave here. And my friends with me."

Barry laughed some more. "I'm so sorry, my friend, but even as we speak, Keith should be cutting up their corpses for dinner tomorrow. I'm afraid they should be very dead by now."

Henry's eyes went wide.

Was this true? Were his friends truly dead? Or was this just Barry trying to bide time while he waited for more of his guards to get the drop on him?

The door to the roof was kicked open and three more guards charged onto the roof. The three men spread out, weapons aimed at Henry's head.

Barry chuckled. "It would seem I have the upper hand, yes?" He glanced to the new arrivals. "If he moves, kill him!" Barry ordered his men. "Well, I suppose I don't need this anymore," he said, looking at Gwen.

While Henry stood helpless, Barry slit Gwen's throat.

She stood on the edge of the roof, her blood shooting out of the jagged wound with every beat of her heart. The wind caught the blood spray and sent it flying over the edge to patter down onto the cement below like red rain.

She stumbled closer to the edge, her foot balancing on the edge for the briefest of moments and then her right foot stepped out into the air and she fell away to plummet the two-stories to the ground below.

Just before she went over, her terror-filled eyes locked with Henry's and he knew she saw him.

Then she was gone.

"Nooo! You bastard!" Henry screamed, his eyes wide with shock. Shooting from the hip with his Glock, he dived for cover. Barry did the same, lunging for the protection of a defunct transformer.

Henry shot round after round at the guards around him, but there were too damn many. With tears distorting his vision from the loss of Gwen, he emptied the last rounds in the shotgun. Throwing it to the roof, he pulled the .357 from his back and started firing.

One shot went straight through the thin metal of the ductwork, killing the man hiding behind it. The guard looked down at the hole in his chest and his face took on one of bemusement. Then he pitched forward into the gravel already soaked with his blood.

The other guards moved further back, finding more solid obstacles to put between themselves and Henry.

A bullet whined by Henry's head, so close he felt the displacement of the air. A barrage followed and he ducked down low to avoid being hit.

He could see Barry's head poking out from behind the transformer, but Henry knew the second he tried to take the man out, he would be shot down by the other guard's bullets.

At the moment, he was in a stalemate, although every fiber of his being wanted to recklessly charge out and kill Barry. Still, he held off. That would be his last option.

"You seem to be trapped, my friend! Your plan did not go as you would have hoped, eh? I tell you what, surrender and I will kill you quick. I promise!" Barry taunted from his hiding place.

Henry answered the man by firing at his position. The bullet hit the graveled roof and became embedded in the tar, the force of the round enough to prevent it from ricocheting. Barry jumped back for cover, his cursing floating over the roof.

"You will pay for that, I promise you!" The man yelled.

Frowning, Henry thought the man may be right. Trapped out on a roof, low on ammunition and surrounded by armed men. His friends were probably dead, and even if he was to escape the roof and somehow manage to get down the side of the building, there were still hundreds of the undead to deal with.

The sound of footsteps on gravel came to him as the guards closed the noose.

Gritting his teeth, he pulled the Glock from its holster and the .357 shifted to his left hand. Holding a weapon in each hand, he readied himself for his last stand.

If he was going down, then he was going to take as many of the bastards with him as he could.

Just before he was ready to attack on his suicide run, shots sounded from behind him. He turned to look, but there were too many obstacles blocking his vision.

Fine, he thought, more for me to kill.

Then he raised himself to his full height and stepped out into the open, weapons firing a barrage of death.

CHAPTER THIRTY

JIMMY, MARY AND CINDY rose with the sun. The three of them sat around the storage room still unsure of how to proceed. A bucket in the corner had the morning's necessities in it, two blankets covering it to control the smell. Numerous suggestions were thrown about, but none seemed sound. Then, from out front in the hallway, they heard the sound of people yelling.

The three quietly made it to the front of the store and through the covered glass they were able to make out parts of the conversations as people rushed past.

Then a group of guards ran by, calling to each other. The lead guard was talking to the others

"Barry wants every man not at the loading dock to get on the roof, they've got that guy, Watson, trapped up there and they need help taking him down." Then the group was past the store and the hallway became quiet again.

Jimmy looked at the women. "Well, you wanted a signal from Henry, there it is," he said.

Mary's face went serious. "We've got to get up there. If we can come from behind, we can hit them before they know we're there."

"Then we should get going, or by the time we get there it won't matter anymore," Cindy stated as she went back to retrieve their weapons.

Mary looked at Jimmy and smiled. "I like her, did I tell you that?"

Jimmy shook his head no. "No, but I had a feeling you two would hit it off. Come on, let's help her and then get out of here. I don't think we have much time."

Less than five minutes later the three friends were on the move.

With all the guards either at the loading dock or on the roof, the companions had no problem moving about the shopping mall. A few residents hastily moved from their path as the three armed warriors charged down the hallways, their footsteps echoing off the walls.

Once they had made it to the stairs, they had to stop. They realized if they wanted to make it to the roof undetected, they would need to find another way, as the roof was guarded by two security guards, the voices of the two men carrying down from above.

They slowly made their way back to the main section of the mall and then discussed alternate ways to reach Henry.

It was Mary who came up with an idea and quickly filled the others in.

Moving through the shopping mall, they stopped at a sporting goods store. While a lot of the merchandise in the store was gone, many of the shelves were still full, the materials not needed yet by the residents. The companions ran through the aisles until Cindy called out to the others.

"I think I found what you wanted," she said.

Jimmy looked at what she was holding. A long coil of rope with knots tied into the line every foot or so. At the end of the rope was a long, three pronged metal hook with a barbed tip. It resembled three giant fishhooks welded together in the middle, only much larger. The grapnel would be exactly what they needed.

"That's great, Cindy," Mary said pleased.

"Not just great, fantastic," Jimmy said, kissing her. "That's exactly what we need. "Come on, let's move." The three left the store at a run, moving through the mall. Their destination was the other end of the complex and time was running out for their friend trapped on the roof.

Seven minutes later, the three companions stopped at the door leading to the stairwell for Barry's office. Jimmy had his .38 in his hands when the three went through the opening. He didn't expect company, but only dead men took chances. Dashing up the stairwell, they quickly covered the distance and were soon standing in front of the closed door of Barry's office.

Kicking the door with the heel of his boot, Jimmy jumped inside the room, ready to blow away any opposition.

The room was empty.

He stood up slowly and placed his weapon back in its holster on the side of his leg. The holster was another acquisition from the supplies of one of the stores. Mary and Cindy followed him into the empty room.

Mary smiled sinfully. "No one for you to shoot at, huh partner?" She joked, looking around the room.

Jimmy turned to look at her. "Yeah, well, better safe than dead."

She nodded. "Point taken, give me a hand with this desk, will you?"

Jimmy moved to help her and together the two of them shifted the desk until it was directly under the skylight. Then Mary grabbed the grapnel and waved the others off.

"All right, get ready for falling glass," she said.

Twirling the rope with the grapnel at the end like she was in the Wild West, Mary tossed the line up to the skylight. But instead of the glass shattering, the grapnel bounced off the skylight and fell back to the floor, making the companions jump out of the way or risk being struck on the head.

Mary placed her hands on her hips and looked up at the skylight.

"Damn, its reinforced glass, this thing won't break it," She said, pointing to the grapnel.

"Makes sense," Jimmy said. "The glass would have to be strong enough to withstand the weight of snow and ice in the winter."

"So what do we do?" Cindy asked.

Suddenly they heard the sound of gunshots filtering in from up above.

Jimmy pulled his .38. "I think that answers your question. Stand back."

The women did as asked and Jimmy put two bullets through the skylight. The first one did nothing but leave a small hole, but the second bullet started a spider web of cracks. But still the skylight held.

"Okay Mary, try again," Jimmy told her, stepping out of the way.

Mary twirled the grapnel again. When she was at the desired speed, she sent it flying up at the skylight. This time the metal hook punched through it, sending pieces of hardened glass raining down onto the companions.

By staying on the edges of the small office, they all managed to avoid all but a few small pieces from striking them. Mary had been hit the most and she now stood over the desk, shaking small pieces of glass from her hair. They rained down to the floor with the sound of crystal.

She checked her arms, with the exception of a few small cuts, she had made it unscathed.

More gunshots floated down from the roof, louder now that the glass was missing, shocking them to action. The grapnel had caught onto something over the lip of the skylight, and after a quick tug to make sure it was secure, Jimmy decided he would be the first up the rope.

After climbing on the desk, he jumped up two more feet. Using both his hands and legs, he shimmied up the rope, using the knots for handholds. Reaching the top of the line, he noticed the grapnel had caught on a heavy piece of metal conduit that ran across the roof from one end to the other

Mary had stayed below, holding the rope steady, and now that he was on the roof, she began climbing while Cindy held the rope for her. Lighter and with a greater muscle mass, thanks to months of living hard on the road, Mary climbed easily. Once at the top, Jimmy was there with a helping hand, and quickly pulled her over the edge.

"Cindy, tie the rifles to the rope and I'll pull them up, then you can come up," Jimmy said from above.

"Okay," she said and then quickly secured the weapons by their trigger guards. Jimmy pulled them up, careful not to let them strike the sides of the skylight. A bent barrel wouldn't do them any good.

Once he had them, he dropped the rope down and Cindy climbed up. Meanwhile, Mary was watching their backs. They were at the south side of the shopping mall, and all the action seeming to be taking place on the north side. There was a lot of roof between them and their quarry; with countless ducts and air conditioning units blocking them from view.

Mary noticed a water tower off to the side. That would explain how they stored water at the mall. She was close to the edge of the roof, and when she looked out across the open landscape, she could see the tip of what appeared to be a lake or reservoir. There was the mall's source for fresh water.

With the cool air blowing on her face, she realized this wasn't a bad place to call home, despite the horrors Barry had unleashed among the oblivious residents.

Cindy was just climbing over the edge of the skylight with Jimmy's help, and once she was up, Mary handed her a rifle. The three of them were armed and ready to move out.

Suddenly, they heard a scream followed by someone yelling no! The three looked at each other.

"That sounded like Henry," Mary said, worry crossing her face.

"If it is, then things just went from bad to worse," Jimmy said. "Come on, let's go. Keep low and wait until we're right behind the bastards. Then hit 'em hard and fast." The two women nodded and they were off.

Slipping from duct to duct to transformer, they made their way across the roof. Rifle shots came to them as the battle between Henry and the guards escalated. Jimmy could hear the sound of a shotgun. None of the guards carried one so that must be Henry. Moving closer, the shotgun stopped to be replaced by the sound of the .357. The loud pop was distinctive and Jimmy had learned to identify it after only hearing it a few times.

Jimmy tossed a piece of gravel at Mary. When she turned to look at him, he used hand signals and told her to go to the left, circling around to catch the guards in the middle. Cindy was next to him and he whispered for her to go right. He would continue moving straight and in less than a minute, they would be ready to join the fight.

Cindy moved off and Jimmy waited a tense thirty seconds for them to get into position, then he moved forward. He was close enough that he could see Henry, but there was no way to warn his friend that help was on the way. He would just have to hope the man figured it out on his own.

Just before he was ready to fire at the closest guard, Henry stepped out into the open with both handguns blazing.

It was now or never.

Jimmy raised his .38 and shot the first guard in the back. The man never knew what hit him as he spit blood and fell to the graveled roof with an exploded chest and a new hole in his torso.

Jimmy continued forward.

There was a guard on his left, and before Jimmy could get off a shot, the man had swiveled on his waist and was shooting at him. Jimmy dived to the roof, gravel scraping his chin. He rolled twice and came up in a crouch with a two-handed grip on the .38. Squeezing the trigger twice in a row, he sent two rounds into the man's chest and stomach.

The guard was thrown back against the air conditioning unit he had used for cover and then slid down to the roof, leaving a bloody smear on the metal behind him. Jimmy didn't see this. Once he knew the man was down, he was already moving tighter into the circle.

In front of him, Henry was shooting from the open, his guns sending bullet after bullet at the guards, keeping them ducking for cover.

Cindy was picking off guards like a sniper. Each time she fired, another man went down. Satisfied her area was secure, she moved a little closer.

Mary had circled around and had shot the only guard she came upon. She was quietly moving across the roof, but the gravel signaled her every move. She turned a corner and a man was standing there. His rifle was aimed toward Henry, ready to shoot him in the back, but at the sound of Mary's footsteps, he swiveled his head in her direction, and she could see he was just as surprised to see her as she was to see him.

But Mary moved a little faster. The guard had to try and bring his weapon around, while all Mary had to do was raise the front end of hers up in the air. She squeezed the trigger, the rifle down at waist level. The weapon bucked slightly in her hands and the guard received a bullet to his neck.

He immediately dropped his rifle, his hands moving to his throat to stop the blood flow, but it was useless. Drowning in his own blood, the guard slumped to the roof. Mary moved forward. She was close to the edge of the roof now and below her was the loading dock. She looked down quickly and saw a Ford F-150 half in and half out of the bay doors. To her right was Henry. He had his back to her and she was about to call out to him when an arm suddenly circled around her neck. Before she knew it, she felt a hard punch to her side that knocked the wind from her lungs and she dropped the rifle. Then she felt the cold metal of a blade against her neck.

Barry pulled her further out from where he'd been hiding and he whispered into her ear. "One false move and I'll cut your throat. And you know I'll do it. Do you understand?"

She nodded her head, but felt the blade cut shallowly into her neck, so she stopped. "Yes, I hear you, you bastard."

He squeezed her throat tighter." Now, now, what did I say about name calling?"

He pulled her to him and turned her to look at him, and when he saw the look in her eyes, he knew he had won, at least for the moment.

"I don't know how you managed to escape the kitchens, but it seems irrelevant at the moment," he said.

Spinning her around, he moved farther onto the roof until he was directly behind Henry. He cursed himself for not having a weapon other than his knife. If he had, he could have put a bullet into the troublesome man's back and ended his problems once and for all.

"All right, I think that's enough play time for now, Mr. Watson! Unless you want a repeat of today, drop you weapons!" Barry yelled to Henry's back.

Henry turned, guns in hand. He had just finished emptying both weapons and was about to consign his soul to Hell when he turned at the sound of his name.

His eyes went wide with shock. He couldn't believe what he was seeing. Not only was Mary alive, but that bastard Barry had her as his prisoner.

It was Gwen all over again.

He lowered his guns. They were empty and useless anyway. A shot sounded from off to his right and another guard fell to the roof with a hole in the side of his head.

Both Jimmy and Cindy moved closer. They had neutralized the last of the guards only to find Mary was captured again. Both Jimmy and Cindy stopped, realizing they needed to let this play out, at least for the immediate moment.

Cindy kneeled down behind a duct. She was trying to line up a shot that would take out Barry, but the man was always hiding too much behind Mary. She didn't feel confident that her shot wouldn't hit Mary, so she waited, hoping for an opening.

"So help me, Barry. If you don't let her go, I will kill you."

"Oh, really, and what if I do let her go? What will you do then?" Barry laughed.

Henry looked back with a humorless smile. "Oh, I'll still kill you, only I promise not to let you suffer, much, anyway."

"I'm sorry, Mr. Watson, but I don't like those choices. What if I kill her and then I kill you? If I'm right, you are out of bullets, otherwise I believe you would have shot me the moment you turned around." He pressed the knife into Mary's throat, eliciting a squeal of pain from her. A small rivulet of blood ran from the knife point to be lost in her cleavage. The front of her shirt started to turn vermilion as the fabric absorbed the blood.

Inside his mind, Henry was fuming in anger. There was no way to get to Barry before he cut her throat. Then he looked into Mary's eyes. She looked at him and she grinned.

He knew that grin.

God help them both, she was going to try something. He wanted to tell her no, that it was too risky, but it was already too late.

Mary slumped in Barry's arms, acting like she had fainted. Not expecting the passive response from the woman, his grip loosened on her, the blade moving away from her throat.

The moment the blade was taken away, Mary went into action. Barry's head was knocked to the side as Mary lunged to her right, her elbow coming up to strike the man in the temple. The knife wavered in his hand, but he held on to it, ready to stab it into Mary's chest.

Henry watched this in slow motion, helpless to stop it. Then he remembered the knife he had kept from one of the guards he'd brought down the day before. Dropping to one knee, he reached into his boot and pulled the blade from its sheath. With a twist of his wrist, he threw the blade at Barry's chest. Unfortunately, he wasn't as skilled as he would have preferred and the blade only struck the man in the shoulder.

Barry cried out from the shallow slice of his flesh from the flying blade, distracted for the half second Mary needed. Mary took a step backward and spun her body in a three-hundred-and-sixty-degree arc, her sneaker spun around in a blur and struck Barry in the chest, kicking the man toward the edge of the roof. His arms flailed as he tried to keep his balance and then he succeeded.

His face went from one of panic to one of triumph when he realized he wasn't going to fall.

Suddenly, a rifle shot rang out and a hole appeared in his chest. The impact of the bullet was enough to push him over the edge. He wavered for another moment, seeming to defy gravity, and then fell to the asphalt below.

The sounds of multiple, dry tree branches breaking floated up to Henry as Barry's legs took the brunt of the fall.

His screaming continued once he hit the ground below. Both of his legs were shattered, the bones punching through his flesh and pants. The sound Henry had heard were Barry's legs shattering from the impact of the fall. Although Barry's pain was unbearable, it was about to become worse.

Ever so slowly, the walking dead surrounded him, his cries for help like a beacon to them. Henry looked down from the roof, Mary in his arms. Barry's face could be seen for only a heartbeat, his agonizing screams echoing off the stone facade of the mall and loading dock.

Hands and teeth dove in and his face was lost among the desiccated bodies. His limbs were torn apart and legs were pulled off as teeth ate away the tissue connecting them. His neck had three sets of teeth chewing on the muscle and skin. Other rotting hands pulled at his head, trying to separate it from the rest of his body. Another set of teeth tore more muscle from his neck allowing the head to tear free. With his mouth still moving in soundless screams, the ghoul carried the head away to feed more privately. Once he was ripped to pieces, the zombie's moved away with their prizes, some of them fighting each other for a bloody gobbet of flesh.

When they finally moved away, there was nothing left but a bloody stain and a few small scraps of gristle. Henry looked down below, but there was no sign of Gwen. What had happened to Barry had happened to her, as well.

Some of the undead gazed up at the companions on the roof with milky white eyes, as if they were waiting for more meat. They had fed well today and wanted more.

And soon they would get more, as the bodies of the dead guards would have to be disposed of. What better way than to toss them off the roof and let them be devoured.

Henry stared at the mess of blood and gore below and he squeezed Mary tighter. The stench was close to overwhelming.

"Before you got here, he killed Gwen," Henry said in a cold voice devoid of emotion. "He threw her off the roof like she was a piece of trash. There was nothing I could do. He just sliced her throat and threw her off."

Mary said nothing, but just stood next to him, holding his hand.

"She was the first woman I was with since Emily died, since all this shit happened," he said, waving his hand across the parking lot and the world in general.

"What do I do now?" Although Mary was next to him, she had the distinct impression he was talking to himself. She watched as a single tear rolled down his cheek.

"Well, you still have us, she said. "You know I love you. And so does Jimmy. Even though he would never say it."

He looked down at her, as if he was seeing her for the first time.

He smiled slightly.

"What do you say we get down from here?" He whispered.

She nodded, agreeing completely.

Henry walked slowly to where he'd dropped his guns. They were empty now, but he still had a few clips for the Glock and there was still a half box of rounds left for the .357 back in the ceiling of their alcove. The shotgun was another thing. At the moment his was empty and Jimmy only had a few shells left loaded in his shotgun still in the ceiling, but not enough to travel the deadlands with. But with luck they would find more ammo down the road. Mary caught up to him after retrieving her rifle and the two started for the roof exit.

Jimmy took one last look over the side of the shopping mall, his eyes glancing at the bloody spot on the asphalt and the milling crowd of undead.

Sending a large blob of phlegm over the side, he took Cindy's hand in his and the two followed the others to the roof access door.

Jimmy smiled and chuckled.

"What's so funny?" Cindy asked.

"What? Oh, I was just thinking how ironic it all was."

"What do you mean?" She asked.

Jimmy's smile grew larger. "Well, here was a man who was killing people and eating them and the man basically died by being eaten himself. That's got to be some kind of poetic justice," he joked.

She thought about it for a moment while they walked across the roof and then she stopped before they reached the door, her hand holding him back.

"You might be right, but let's keep it to ourselves, okay?"

He nodded. "Yeah, that's probably a good idea."

With the sounds of the dead rising over the shopping mall, the companions went back inside.

Above the roof, the crows flew overhead, eyeing the dead guards, waiting for their chance to feed, too.

CHAPTER THIRTY-ONE

THE COMPANIONS WALKED down the stairwell in silence, Henry's mood a pall over them all. Although Barry was dead, they still had no idea of the reception the other residents would give them.

The truth was, their fight could be far from over.

Jimmy poked his head out into the hallway to see how safe it was.

There were two guards standing watch. With his .38 in hand, Jimmy stepped out of the stairwell, followed by the others.

At the sounds of the companion's footsteps, the guards turned to look at them. But instead of leveling their rifles, they raised their hands in surrender.

"Wait," the man on his right said. "We're not your enemy! Don't shoot!"

"Oh really, And why is that?" Jimmy said, his .38 still leveled with the guard's chest.

"We heard that Barry's dead. And so is the security chief. All the people who wanted you dead are dead themselves. We were never part of that shit. We just did what they told us. We don't care what you do, as long as you're not going to threaten the mall or the residents," the first guard said.

The other stood next to him, hardily nodding his head in agreement to everything his friend was saying.

"What's your name, son?" Henry said, pushing his way next to Jimmy.

"Adam, sir."

"Well, Adam, unless you know of someone better, I'd say you're in charge of this mall," Henry told him

"Me?" Adam said. "But why?"

Henry smiled, although the smile didn't reach his eyes. "Why? That's easy. You already answered your own question. Because everyone else is dead."

A crowd was starting to gather around the companions and a heavy set man with a balding head and two chins pushed his way to the front.

Jimmy turned with his gun in hand. The man raised his hands and smiled, weakly.

"Whoa there, boy, I'm a friend, don't shoot." He looked at Henry and waited for the warrior to look at him.

"I'm Gene. I was a friend of Gwen's. She told me what was happening and asked me to help you in any way I can. She told me what Barry and his buddies had done. Hell, it's still hard to believe. At first I didn't want to, but I went to the kitchens. I went to the rooms that Barry only let certain people have access to. Good God, I can't believe what I found. Shit, it makes the damn rotters seem almost human."

Jimmy had lowered his gun, although he still kept it in his hand.

Gene saw this and moved a little closer.

"Look, the people around here know me and respect me. Let's get you people some place you can rest. Then give me some time to spread the word about what's happened. Once that's done, you can walk around here without looking over your shoulder. What do you say?"

Henry looked to Jimmy and then at the women. All three nodded in agreement.

Henry turned back to Gene.

"Well, Gene, I don't see that we really have a choice, so yes, thank you. That sounds wonderful."

Gene turned and started to push his way back through the crowd. "Excellent, follow me and I'll escort you back to your berths," the large man said. "Come on, people get out of the way, these people are friends! I'll explain it later. Community meeting in one hour in the food court; spread it around!" Gene yelled to the surrounding crowd.

As Henry started moving, he slowed and called out to Adam again, waving the man to him. The young guard moved into the line and followed Henry and the others down the hall.

"What about the loading dock, what's the status?" Henry asked.

"With the exception of the rotters being inside, it's secure. The main doors are holding, they're solid metal or close to it," Adam said, moving next to Henry.

Henry nodded. "Up on the roof, behind the farthest a/c unit is the control box for the pinger. Go get it. Once you turn it on, most, if not all of the crowd should go to it like before. When they do, go out there and take out any stragglers and get the truck that's sticking out back inside. And do it now."

Adam nodded. "Yes, sir. If I have any questions, can I come to you?"

"Sure, kid, no problem," Henry said. Then Adam disappeared into the crowd of people. It seemed the whole complex was coming out to see what the commotion was. Henry just hoped there wasn't a guard left who was loyal to Barry who wanted to get a little revenge. But as they moved through the mall that seemed more and more unlikely.

When they were finally at their quarters again, Henry noticed all signs of his fight to the death with Barry's enforcer were gone.

That suited him just fine.

"Go ahead and crash, I'll take first watch," Jimmy said to Henry as he dropped into a chair near the door.

"Do you really think that's necessary?" Cindy asked.

Jimmy shrugged. "Probably not. I think everybody that wanted to cause us harm is either dead or in a deader's stomach. But I'm not taking chances."

Mary nodded, "Makes sense. Tell you what. Wake me in two hours and I'll relieve you." She walked over to Jimmy and kissed him on the cheek.

Jimmy touched his hand to his cheek and looked up at her curiously. "What was that for?"

She smiled. "That, my friend, was just for being you." She smiled at Cindy and then went into the back of their alcove to be with Henry.

Stepping into the back, she saw Henry sitting in the corner of the small room. He was just sitting there staring at the wall. She walked over and slid down next to him, placing her head on his shoulder.

"What'cha doin'?" She asked, softly.

He shrugged, her head moving with the movement. "Thinking, I guess."

"Can I ask about what?"

He sighed heavily. "Mostly about Gwen, how things might have been with her. You know, I think I could have been happy with her, really happy."

"I know. I'm so sorry about the way things worked out," Mary said.

The two of then sat quietly for more than fifteen minutes, neither of them talking.

Then Henry broke the silence. "That was a pretty good trick you pulled up on the roof. Where the hell did you learn that?"

She smiled and sat up. "Well, the moves were some of the things you've taught me over the past few months, and as for the trick to faint and then hit him. Well…" She trailed off.

"Yes, come on, spit it out," he cajoled her.

"Well, that I got from a movie I saw a year ago."

His eyes opened wide. "Your kidding, a movie? Are you crazy, do know what could have happened if it hadn't worked?"

She nodded. "Yes, Henry, I think I do. It was my neck he had that knife to, you know," she said with her eyes flaring with anger.

He saw how upset she was becoming and tried to calm her down. "I'm sorry, but gees, a movie? Promise me you won't do anything crazy like that again."

She hesitated for a moment, then nodded. "If it will make you feel better, then okay. I promise."

"You don't mean it," he said.

"All right, I promise the next time I'm on a rooftop and a crazy man has a knife to my throat, that I'll let you handle it. Okay, is that better?"

He laughed and this time it went all the way to his eyes, "Yes, that's better, now come here."

She leaned back against him and sighed, the discussion over.

"It's just that it was bad enough I lost Gwen. I had only known her for a few days, but if I lost you, well, I don't know what I'd do. You're the daughter I never had. You're my only family left. Well, you and Jimmy, as scary as that seems."

"I heard that, right back atcha', you old bastard," Jimmy joked from out front. "And don't forget Cindy, she's part of the family, too."

Henry chuckled. "You didn't give me a chance. And Cindy, too, now quit eavesdropping and go stand watch," Henry called playfully.

From the front room, Henry and Mary could hear Cindy chastising Jimmy. He liked the blonde woman, she was a good influence on Jimmy.

Henry leaned back and sighed again.

They remained quiet, and soon, despite the sun shining outside, they fell asleep in each others arms.

For now they were safe from the undead and had a roof over their heads. Whatever the future would hold for the four companions, they would face it as a family.

With weapons cocked and loaded.

THE NEXT EXCITING CHAPTER IN THE DEADWATER SERIES!

DEADWAVE
By Anthony Giangregorio

Henry Watson was an ordinary man with an ordinary life.

He had a wife, a job and friends who loved him.

But then the rains came. Clouds filled with deadly bacteria that fell from the sky to change people into flesh-eating ghouls.

With no past and an uncertain future, Henry and his companions travel the deadlands of what was once America, searching for someplace safe, devoid of an undead presence. But the world has changed and it is very possible there is nowhere safe, from either man or zombie.

After spending the winter in a shopping mall with other survivors of the zombie apocalypse, the political climate grows uneasy and the companions decide its time to leave; traveling south.

Meanwhile, in Connecticut, an ex-crime boss has taken over a submarine base, and with a nuclear submarine at his disposal, hopes to shape an empire out of the ashes of America.

The flame of hope may dwindle, but the will to survive burns bright.

DEAD RECKONING: DAWNING OF THE DEAD
By Anthony Giangregorio

THE DEAD HAVE RISEN!

In the dead city of Pittsburgh, two small enclaves struggle to survive, eking out an existence of hand to mouth.

But instead of working together, both groups battle for the last remaining fuel and supplies of a city filled with the living dead.

Six months after the initial outbreak, a lone helicopter arrives bearing two more survivors and a newborn baby. One enclave welcomes them, while the other schemes to steal their helicopter and escape the decaying city.

With no police, fire, or social services existing, the two will battle for dominance in the steel city of the walking dead.

But when the dust settles, the question is: will the remaining humans be the winners, or the losers?

When the dead walk, the line between Heaven and Hell is so twisted and bent there is no line at all.

RISE OF THE DEAD
By Anthony Giangregorio

DEATH IS ONLY THE BEGINNING

In less than forty-eight hours, more than half the globe was infected.
In another forty-eight, the rest would be enveloped.
The reason?
A science experiment gone horribly wrong which enabled the dead to walk, their flesh rotting on their bones even as they seek human prey.

Jeremy was an ordinary nineteen year old slacker. He partied too much and had done poorly in high school. After a night of drinking and drugs, he awoke to find the world a very different place from the one he'd left the night before. The dead were walking and feeding on the living, and as Jeremy stepped out into a world gone mad, the dead spotting him alone and unarmed in the middle of the street, he had to wonder if he would live long enough to see his twentieth birthday.

BOOK 6

DEAD UNION

By Anthony Giangregorio

BRAVE NEW WORLD

More than a year has passed since the world died not with a bang, but with a moan.

Where sprawling cities once stood, now only the dead inhabit the hollow walls of a shattered civilization; a mockery of lives once led.

But there are still survivors in this barren world, all slowly struggling to take back what was stripped from their birthright; the promise of a world free of the undead.

Fortified towns have shunned the outside world, becoming massive fortresses in their own right. These refugees of a world torn asunder are once again trying to carve out a new piece of the earth, or hold onto what little they already possess.

HOSTAGES

Henry Watson and his warrior survivalists are conscripted by a mad colonel, one of the last military leaders still functioning in the decimated United States. The colonel has settled in Fort Knox, and from there plans to rule the world with his slave army of lost souls and the last remaining soldiers of a defunct army.

But first he must take back America and mold it in his own image; and he will crush all who oppose him, including the new recruits of Henry and crew.

The battle lines are drawn with the fate of America at stake, and this time, the outcome may be unsure.

In a world where the dead walk, even the grave isn't safe.

THE DARK

By Anthony Giangregorio

DARKNESS FALLS

The darkness came without warning.

First New York, then the rest of United States, and then the world became enveloped in a perpetual night without end.

With no sunlight, eventually the planet will wither and die, bringing on a new Ice Age. But that isn't problem for the human race, for humanity will be dead long before that happens.

There is something in the dark, creatures only seen in nightmares, and they are on the prowl.

Evolution has changed and man is no longer the dominant species.

When we are children, we are told not to fear the dark, that what we believe to exist in the shadows is false.

Unfortunately, that is no longer true.

DARK PLACES
By Anthony Giangregorio

A cave-in inside the Boston subway unleashes something that should have stayed buried forever.

Three boys sneak out to a haunted junkyard after dark and find more than they gambled on.

In a world where everyone over twelve has died from a mysterious illness, one young boy tries to carry on.

A mysterious man in black tries his hand at a game of chance at a local carnival, to interesting results.

God, Allah, and Buddha play a friendly game of poker with the fate of the Earth resting in the balance.

Ever have one of those days where everything that can go wrong, does? Well, so did Byron, and no one should have a day like this!

Thad had an imaginary friend named Charlie when he was a child. Charlie would make him do bad things. Now Thad is all grown up and guess who's coming for a visit?

These and other short stories, all filled with frozen moments of dread and wonder, will keep you captivated long into the night.

Just be sure to watch out when you turn off the light!

ROAD KILL: A ZOMBIE TALE
By Anthony Giangregorio

ORDER UP!

In the summer of 2008, a rogue comet entered earth's orbit for 72 hours. During this time, a strange amber glow suffused the sky.

But something else happened; something in the comet's tail had an adverse affect on dead tissue and the result was the reanimation of every dead animal carcass on the planet.

A handful of survivors hole up in a diner in the backwoods of New Hampshire while the undead creatures of the night hunt for human prey.

There's a new blue plate special at DJ's Diner and Truck Stop, and it's you!

THE MONSTER UNDER THE BED
By Anthony Giangregorio

Rupert was just one of many monsters that inhabit the human world, scaring children before bed. Only Rupert wanted to play with the children he was forced to scare.

When Rupert meets Timmy, an instant friendship is born. Running away from his abusive step-father, Timmy leaves home, embarking on a journey that leads him to New York City.

On his way, Timmy will realize that the true monsters are other adults who are just waiting to take advantage of a small boy, all alone in the big city.

Can Rupert save him?

Or will Timmy just become another statistic.

SOULEATER
By Anthony Giangregorio

Twenty years ago, Jason Lawson witnessed the brutal death of his father by something only seen in nightmares, something so horrible he'd blocked it from his mind.

Now twenty years later the creature is back, this time for his son.

Jason won't let that happen.

He'll travel to the demon's world, struggling every second to rescue his son from its clutches.

But what he doesn't know is that the portal will only be open for a finite time and if he doesn't return with his son before it closes, then he'll be trapped in the demon's dimension forever.

DEAD TALES: SHORT STORIES TO DIE FOR
By Anthony Giangregorio

In a world much like our own, terrorists unleash a deadly dis-ease that turns people into flesh-eating ghouls.

A camping trip goes horribly wrong when forces of evil seek to dominate mankind.

After losing his life, a man returns reincarnated again and again; his soul inhabiting the bodies of animals.

In the Colorado Mountains, a woman runs for her life, stalked by a sadistic killer.

In a world where the Patriot Act has come to fruition, a man struggles to survive, despite eroding liberties.

Not able to accept his wife's death, a widower will cross into the dream realm to find her again, despite the dark forces that hold her in thrall.

These and other short stories will captivate and thrill you. These are short stories to die for.

DEADFREEZE
By Anthony Giangregorio

THIS IS WHAT HELL WOULD BE LIKE IF IT FROZE OVER.

When an experimental serum for hypothermia goes horribly wrong, a small research station in the middle of Antarctica becomes overrun with an army of the frozen dead.

Now a small group of survivors must battle the arctic weather and a horde of frozen zombies as they make their way across the frozen plains of Antarctica to a neighboring research station.

What they don't realize is that they are being hunted by an entity whose sole reason for existing is vengeance; and it will find them wherever they run.

DEADFALL
By Anthony Giangregorio

It's Halloween in the small suburban town of Wakefield, Mass.

While parents take their children trick or treating and others throw costume parties, a swarm of meteorites enter the earth's atmosphere and crash to earth.

Inside are small parasitic worms, no larger than maggots.

The worms quickly infect the corpses at a local cemetery and so begins the rise of the undead.

The walking dead soon get the upper hand, with no one believing the truth.

That the dead now walk.

Will a small group of survivors live through the zombie apocalypse?

Or will they, too, succumb to the Deadfall.

DEAD HARVEST

By Anthony Giangregorio

Lost at sea and fearing for their lives, a miracle arrives on the horizon, in the shape of a cruise ship, saving Henry Watson and his friends from a watery grave.

Enjoying the safety of the commandeered ship, Henry and his companions take a much needed rest and settle down for a life at sea, but after a devastating storm sends the companions adrift once again, they find themselves separated, exhausted, and washed ashore on the coast of California.

With each person believing the others in the group are dead; they fall into the middle of a feud between two neighboring towns, the companions now unknowingly battling against one another.

Needing to escape their newfound prisons, each one struggles to adapt to their new life, while the tableau of life continues around them.

But one sadistic ruler will seek to unleash the awesome power of the living dead on his unsuspecting adversaries, wiping the populace from the face of the earth, and in doing so, take Henry and his friends with them.

Though death looms around every corner, man's journey is far from over.

LIVING DEAD PRESS

Where the Dead Walk

www.livingdeadpress.com

Book One of the *Undead World Trilogy*

BLOOD
OF THE
DEAD

A Shoot 'Em Up Zombie Novel by A.P. Fuchs

"*Blood of the Dead* . . . is the stuff
of nightmares . . . with some
unnerving and frightening action
scenes that will have you on the
edge of your seat."

- Rick Hautala
author of *The Wildman*

Joe Bailey prowls the Haven's streets, taking them back from
the undead, each kill one step closer to reclaiming a life once
stolen from him.

As the dead push into the Haven, he and a couple others are
forced into the one place where folks fear to tread: the heart
of the city, a place overrun with flesh-eating zombies.

Welcome to the end of all things.

**Ask for it at your local bookstore.
Also available from your favorite on-line retailer.**

ISBN-10   1-897217-80-3 / ISBN-13   978-1-897217-80-1

www.undeadworldtrilogy.com

Printed in the United States
146960LV00004B/36/P

9 781935 458081